+
St71h

Half Nelson,
Full Nelson

Half Nelson, Full Nelson

Bruce Stone

HARPER & ROW, PUBLISHERS

Library of Congress Cataloging in Publication Data
Stone, Bruce.
    Half Nelson, full Nelson.

    Summary: When his parents separate, Nelson and his
friend Heidi concoct a plan to kidnap Nelson's little
sister and bring his family back together.
    [1. Family problems—Fiction. 2. Divorce—Fiction]
I. Title.
PZ7.S875945Hal 1985   [Fic]   85-42623
ISBN 0-06-025921-3
ISBN 0-06-025922-1 (lib. bdg.)

to the memory of Elizabeth B. Stone
and for Braden

Half Nelson,
Full Nelson

1

I'm Nelson Gato. The Gato part was my dad's last name until he added the r to become the Gator Man. He decided on Nelson because he thought it would be a good name for a wrestler's kid. He used to call me Half Nelson until I got to be taller than him. Matter of fact, he still calls me that sometimes. Big joke.

I live in a trailer park on the highway just before it turns into four lanes and takes you on the Palmetto bypass into Sarasota. The trailer park is my grandmother's little pot of gold. She's had the land over twenty years. Laid down some concrete slabs and power hookups, and she's been in business ever since. She calls it the Gate o' Palms, which really means Gato Palms. The o' part is like the o' part in Land o' Lakes, Bit o' Honey, Chock Full o' Nuts. She's proud of that name, just like she's proud of the four palms she managed to twist and bend until they grew into this fancy

3

archway at the entrance to the park. The trailers all look a little bit like Saltine Boxes, but once you stick on all the garages, carports and breezeways, and scatter a few of those birdbaths and plastic flamingos around, it's just like any other neighborhood. Of course, some people still act like you've got leprosy when you tell them where you live.

The biggest thing to happen around here, except for a few hurricanes, was the day Teddy Delgado drove his beer truck into the side of Helen Neery's trailer. He thought her cats were putting sand in his gas tank. Last I heard old Ted had been shipped off to Chattahoochee. I guess he's being rehabilitated—like me.

Before I turned to crime and General Lee latched on to my dad and made him into the Gator Man, the most famous guy this side of Palmetto was the Green Man. The story goes that when he was a boy he was struck by lightning. Turned him all gray and his hair turned green, just like in these little clay planters where you fill up this guy's head with dirt and then plant grass seed. A week later you get a leprechaun, with green hair poking its way out of the little holes all over his scalp.

But the Green Man is for real. He walks up and down the same stretch of highway every night like he's advertising. When there's nothing better to do everyone likes to cruise the highway just to check him out. They say he's waiting to be zapped by another lightning bolt so that he'll turn back to normal. But Gram says that lightning never strikes the same guy twice, and besides, his brains were probably fried enough the first time around.

So that just leaves the General and the Gator Man—and me.

2

Jungle Fever is what General Lee made out of twenty acres of swamp that used to lie off the old dirt road going out to the town gravel pits. In those days it was mostly the unofficial town dump. People heaped their old tires out there before they found out it was smarter to sell them to the orange groves for burning during the heavy frosts. After that the only thing the swamp was any good for was breeding mosquitoes, but the town even caught on to that and started spraying oil out there when the wrigglers started showing up.

So by the time the General came along the swamp didn't exactly look like choice real estate; even the skeeters were gone, and most of the rats booked for Miami. After he bought it, the bulldozers moved in and smeared some mud around, and then they drained it and filled it in with sand and *clean fill*, which means garbage that doesn't rot and smell. Pretty soon it looked more like a golf course than a swamp, and signs started showing up along the roadsides from as far as Fort Myers and Dade County. The signs were just these huge school-bus-yellow billboards with JUNGLE FEVER spelled across the top. There was a python draped around each word, just like this:

(It's contagioussssssssssssssss)
Just off Highway 93, near Palmetto

Now, you got to admit that's pretty convincing advertising, especially with all those extra *s*'s hissing at you like some killer hognose rattler ready to pounce.

Come opening day, the General was standing right there at the main entrance all dressed up in khaki bush pants and a pith helmet just like he was fresh back from an African safari. He was handing out free shrunken heads to all the kiddies, and Vanessa immediately put hers around her neck, like she'd just made Jaycees in Borneo or something.

Vanessa is my sister. Mom called her Vanessa because she thought it might help her grow up to be a movie star. Of course, Vanessa was only seven and couldn't make very intelligent judgments about things like shrunken heads. It didn't seem to make any difference, neither, when I told her they were really made in Hong Kong out of latex and goat hair, and sold in Woolworth's for 79¢.

So anyhow, me and Dad and Vanessa started following all these bumpy gravel paths around Jungle Fever. There were little plywood arrows stuck alongside the paths, just in case you forgot which direction you were walking in. We had begged Mom to come along, but she was in one of her "I can't stand living like this" moods. Besides, she said, if she really wanted to see a bunch of snakes all she had to do was sign up for her high school reunion, Madeira Pines Class of '59.

Too bad, because Mom would have at least liked the bird section. There were toucans with their hooked canoe bills, and huge macaws from Brazil that looked hand painted, and parrots, smaller and duller than the macaws. Flamingos, real ones, stood on one and two legs in a sort of lagoon pond, like they just grew out of the mud. And peacocks paraded and hissed like angry cats, and even a couple of bald eagles cocked their heads in this sort of separate caged-in penthouse, posing like in some commercial for U.S. Savings Bonds. It wasn't until Vanessa finally saw the vultures ripping chunks of red flesh off some former animal's hindquarters that she decided to move on.

But the real sleazy part was when we got to the monkey house. Dad said the problem with monkeys is that they don't care who's watching—the only difference between us and them is hang-ups. I can usually handle it when all they do is stick their finger in their nose, or check each other for head lice. It's the other stuff that gets a little strong. Especially the baboons. Everything is red and pink and sticking out on one side or the other. Dad said he'd rather see them on TV, where they all wear dresses and pants and the smell isn't so bad. I suppose I agree.

If you're looking for the big moment of destiny that finally led me into a life of crime, I figure what happened next is probably where it all began. We had made it to the alligator pit, which was actually this sunken concrete pond full of swamp ooze and murky green water. And alligators. In the

7

middle of the pond was a concrete island with a ramp spi-raling down into the water. It was like a bigger version of those little plastic dishes, with the island and the plastic palm tree stuck in the middle, where you put baby turtles with flowers painted on their backs. I had one when I was a kid, but the turtle did a cannonball off the island one day, landed on his back and drowned. Mrs. Neery's cats had him for dinner. All except the shell, of course.

The important thing about this gator pit was that it had a wall around it that hit me about waist high. They must have figured it was high enough to keep out the little kids, and besides, the gators ten or twelve feet down there in the pit were not exactly known for their jumping skills. So when Dad asked us to give him a little brother-sister pose by the gator pit, it wasn't like a personal invitation to the jaws of doom just because we decided to sit on that wall.

Problem was that Vanessa thought that was too average—so she stood on the wall while I wrapped my arm loosely around her ankles. Then *click whirrrrrrr*, and the camera shoots out this picture, just like sticking out your tongue. I walked over to watch the picture develop, but before we could even read the "Adidas" on my T-shirt, we heard a kind of muffled scream, like it was half underwater: "Daddyyyy." It was Vanessa!

When we got to the wall we could see that, no matter how she had fallen in, Vanessa was lying belly-down in the mud, propped up on her elbows and screaming for all she was worth. The nearest gator was buried in the ooze about twelve feet away, looking more confused than anything. He blinked a couple times and then started very slowly to just sort of slither over to where Vanessa was wallowing around. That was all Dad needed to see before he vaulted the wall and landed—*whomp*—feetfirst in the mud beside her. He pulled her to standing and pushed her behind him, against the wall.

The gator was getting closer, accelerating. Now, every good Florida boy knows that if you're going to mess with a gator you'd better get there first and hope the gator don't start flashing his gums. So Dad comes at the gator from sideways and kind of throws a full nelson on his snout, locking his jaws shut between both forearms. That's when Dad goes into his famous whirlybird spin, the same move he used to put away Mad Anton the Hun in Panama City. Only now he whirls the gator by the jaws at his waist, not above his head, and after about four good spins he slings the gator some twenty feet across the pit to where it lands and then slides another five feet into a batch of mud and decides to stay put.

A crowd had gathered around the pit, and they all gave a big ringside cheer when the gator landed. But Dad wasn't playing this one to the crowd. He grabbed Vanessa and boosted her up to where I could grab her by the wrists and pull her out. Dad was another story. He was too far down to reach, and too heavy to pull out even if I could. I yelled for some rope, and some of the General's boys shot off in all directions like waterbugs in a rainstorm.

Down in the pit the word seemed to be spreading among the gators that they had company. A big bull gator kind of shivered and slid into the water, his tail dragging behind like a dead vine as he swam toward my dad. Dad circled away from him, his back against the pit wall, and the gator curled toward him, waggling his body side to side, coming faster.

Dad shoots a glance up at the crowd. Standing shoulder to shoulder, bending over the wall, some point at the gator, some throw french fries. Still no rope. The gator's jaws were apart—half-mast, dull teeth thick as spark plugs, some rusty brown, some green like algae. They were close now, almost spitting distance.

Dad goes into his crouch. That's how he started his matches, with that same crouch and the stare from under his eyebrows. He was ready, edging closer. THE KANGAROO! Almost straight up, but with enough push to get him over the jaws, just as the gator lunges. He lands on top with his best banzai yell, half rebel whoop, *AAYYYYYYYUHOOOL*, and you could hear the breath whoosh out of that gator, loud as the air brakes on a sixteen-wheeler. Then he spins around, straddles the old gator, and grabs it under the neck where the jaw hinges together. He gives it his best four-alarm headlock, then stands it straight up and flips its tail underneath, taking away the leverage.

Some guy with Abe Lincoln's chin whiskers finally showed up with the rope just then. I grabbed it from him and tied a big slipknot loop in one end and dropped it down to where Dad and the gator were thrashing around. "Get a leg in there, and get away!" I yelled down into the pit. Dad pinned the gator against the wall where the loop was hanging and somehow managed to wiggle its left front leg in after about three tries. I pulled the rope taut and the loop caught snug around that leg. Me and Abe Lincoln and a couple other guys grabbed hold for the big pull. As soon as Dad felt the gator sliding up the wall, he gave a big heave and slung the gator off to one side. Before that gator slung back down the other way like some green scaly pendulum, Dad had jumped clear of its jaws and stood watching the gator dangling in midair by its armpit. We gave the gator another tug and then lashed the rope around a concrete bench so the gator could think about it. Abe produced a knife and cut off the loose end of the rope. We threw that end over the wall, to where Dad was standing. He turned for a last look. The rest of the gators were at a safe distance, trying to look like they were just waiting for a bus or something. Dad blew them a kiss, grabbed the rope, and walked up the wall like a heavyweight Spiderman.

When he came over the top, the General was waiting there for him. "Bravo!" he says, slipping this huge revolver back into his bush khakis. But my dad says nothing, just slumps down against the wall like he's finished the biggest match of his life. Pretty soon Vanessa's over there with him, and they're hugging, saying nothing. That's when I went over, just so everyone would know they belong with me. I was even going to get in on the hugging, but I decided maybe it was okay to just be there beside them. And besides, it sort of smelled like father-daughter day for the Creatures from the Living Swamp.

3

Some scenes in the following chapter may not be suitable for reading by a child. Parental discretion is advised.

How's that for a grabber? It's like those gas stations where they used to put this big sign outside: "NAKED WOMEN AND SEX (are nice but all we have here is gas for sale and friendly attendants)." I suppose certain demented types get a chuckle out of that, and maybe it even sold a gallon or two of gas—at least in the days before they sold gas gift-wrapped in special holiday decanters.

The problem is we're coming to the Big Blowup. So we get home from Jungle Fever. Vanessa makes the shower. I hide in the bedroom. Dad's in the living room trying to explain. You can almost feel the trailer beginning to shake.

"*Alligators—you mean living, alive . . . ALLIGATORS?* For the love of . . . My baby in a mudpit . . . You almost let my baby get eaten by a bunch of—of—" Whenever Mother got mad she would always start calling Vanessa a baby. She was scorching now, and there was no way out. Dad just tried to keep his voice steady.

"Sherry, honey, it's all right. The General's got ideas for us. Wants to manage me, says he can get me on TV, wants me to do exhibitions on the weekend. It could be good, you know, more money. Get this—he says I should call myself the Gator Man, says Johnny Gato's boring, too much like an everyday kind of name."

"Johnny Gato's dumb as dog waste, that's what Johnny Gato is." She was almost screaming now, close to a nine on the Richter scale. "Get off the carpet. Get in the kitchen. You're nothing but filth. Take your clothes off and throw them outside. I don't need more filth in my life. And stop your pouting."

"I'm not pouting, princess." Mom didn't like being called princess.

"You are so pouting, and your mother's next door with her hearing aid turned up to ten, and in five minutes she'll be over here holding your hand, WON'T YOU, GRAMSIE DEAR?" She was yelling out the window, across the drive to where Gram's trailer sat beside ours. Gram didn't wear a hearing aid; her ears were good. In the past month the police had been out twice to cool things off, and Mom always suspected it was Gram who'd called them.

I heard the door slam. I could see Dad by the front steps, peeling off his mud-caked clothes, stripping right down to his undertrous. He was near 270 pounds and built like a sea lion with feet. His head went straight down into his neck without stopping until it got to his shoulders—some guys called him a no-neck goon, but that was just wrestling talk. He had humongous arms that reached almost to his knees and this massive inflated chest that you could have played handball off of. It all started sloping in at the waist and down along his tapering legs until you got to these two little pixie feet, a dainty size nine if you want to check your program.

"I'm clean now, no more gator poop." Vanessa came blasting out of the bathroom with a cloud of steam rolling right out behind her. Mom followed her into our bedroom with a Holly Hobbie towel as big as a blanket. She wrapped the towel around Vanessa and held her in her lap, drying her hair with a corner of the towel.

"Do you think Daddy will be in the newspaper tomorrow?" Vanessa asked.

"Yeah, babe, maybe in the obituary," Mom said, more to herself.

"What's the bitchery? Is that like the sports page?"

"No, Ness, that's where they put about all the people who die. Mommy was making sort of a joke," I tried to explain.

"Don't you think Daddy will be famous? General Lee said he could be a Gator Man on TV," Vanessa said.

"Mr. Lee probably thinks he can make a lot of money off your father. Everybody makes money off your father except your father. They want him to be a dancing chicken, like up at Webb's City." Mom was talking about this big store in St. Pete where they used to have a chicken that would come out of its cage and sort of scratch around on a turntable to "Turkey in the Straw" every time you put a quarter in the slot. There was also a rabbit that played basketball and a duck that hit home runs.

"Gonna sit out here all night, big Gator Man? Shower's in here if you want to join the living," Mom yelled out the window. She was waggling her fingers through Vanessa's

14

hair, fluffing it out to dry faster. "There, hon, you're all done." She gave Vanessa a little pat on the rump. "Now go get dressed. We're going out."

About a minute later Dad slams the door behind him and goes right to the bathroom. He's still in the shower when Mom and Vanessa get in the Chevy and rumble out the driveway with the exhaust wagging like the tail on a dalmatian.

4

Before you go jumping to conclusions, I suppose I should tell you right off that you shouldn't go getting the wrong impression of my mother. It's just that she's been trying for so long to get my dad to "settle down," which for her means to make up his mind to do one thing for longer than three months at a time. He's been wrestling off and on ever since the navy, when they used to set up matches so he could cream all these poor guys on the one weekend a month when the base movie was a rerun. Mom always says the problem was that when he gave up on the navy he should have given up the wrestling, too. That was fifteen years ago. But instead, he always managed to get a match here and a match there, just enough for a paycheck and a couple bags of groceries. Figured if he could just hook on with a tour, get a manager, make a "name" with a few good connections, maybe he could make it go. Only it never happened. Every few months he'd get a call from a promoter in Miami or Tampa or Jacksonville, or sometimes from Alabama or Georgia. They would usually need a fill-in or a last-minute replacement, and somebody had told them that Johnny Gato always put on a good show and maybe he was available. And he always was.

But in the past few years they called less and less. That's when Mom started getting angry, started putting the heat on. And Dad tried. For a while he was digging foundations, pouring concrete. Then he gave that up to put in swimming pools for the Marvel Pool Company, only they folded. He put tar on houses for a roofing company but hated the stink and the heat and the steam and the sweat in his eyes. Said it was too early yet to be in hell, he had all eternity to be there, no need to rush it. For a while he tried to stick it out at the phosphate mine over by Bartow, but it was a long, dusty day, and he'd come home looking pale as the Doughboy and coughing up little orange balls of spit. And then there would be that one more call, just one final match. That's when Mom laid down the law. She would go into her "I can't stand living like this" speech and threaten to leave if Dad ever stepped into a ring again. The last blowup had been over four months earlier. Dad had promised to try, and was now mostly helping out around the Gate o' Palms, picking sandspurs and painting all the curbstones white. He kept telling us he was looking for something "suitable," but I guess I knew all along there would never be anything "suitable" enough. No surprise, then, at the big shaboo when Dad comes home and tells about General Lee, and about his magical transformation into the Gator Man.

"Here, boy, scrape these good and then use some sandpaper to rough 'em up." Dad threw his size-nine Everlast high tops into my lap. He had been wrestling in the same

17

pair for as long as I could remember, although he must have gone through a pair of laces every year. They tended to rot, what with mildew and all, and the longer they sat the quicker they rotted, especially locked up in that big metal footlocker left over from his navy days. I pulled out my pocketknife and started scraping off the old lumps of resin and pine tar that had grown and blackened there from earlier matches. Dad liked to have good traction for all his kangaroo leaps and flying scissors, and nothing made you look more like a lunt than when you started slingshotting back and forth against the ropes, lost your footing and did a hook slide into the little old ladies in the front row.

"Hurry it up, Nelson. The General said be there by eleven," Dad said, puffing. He was doing sprints across the courtyard, falling into a spasm of somersaults and cartwheels at the end of each sprint, the way a swimmer does flip turns at the end of each lap. Finally he collapsed on the grass beside my chair. He took five deep breaths like a dying vacuum cleaner and spun over onto his back, arching himself up on his heels and the crown of his head— neck bridges, he could do them all day. His face was as red as a blood blister, his neck pumped up like an inner tube. Veins danced alongside his swollen neck like snakes trapped beneath his skin. This getting ready was what filled Dad up the most; sometimes it seemed like the only thing that mattered.

"Mom coming?" I asked, pretty much knowing the answer all along. Mom and Vanessa hadn't been around much since the Big Blowup three days before. Gone here and there every day. No one knew where, and no one dared to ask.

"No . . . not . . . coming." He strained between breaths. "Pissants, damn little pissant things"—and Dad jumped

18

straight up into the air shaking his head and banging at his ears with the heel of his palms. Red ants, ornery or stupid, they'd crawl into just about anything they could. Dad poked around with his little finger.

"There, contemplate that," he said as he smashed the ant against the sharp edge of his thumbnail. "I expect your mother's pretty much through with us, Nelson. Wants me to roll over and play dead, start acting like a grown-up. Keeps telling me I'm a man with a wife and two children, like that's some big miracle never before accomplished in the entire history of the world. This might be the last chance."

"Maybe it's already too late. Ness has been talking about Georgia again," I admitted, referring to our Aunt Ruthie, who lived somewhere up north of Atlanta. She never came to visit, but every time things got tense Mom would threaten to take off for Ruthie's.

"Your mother thinks she can blackmail me into being ordinary just by talk like that. Puke. I've tried, only thing I learned was I'll never be ordinary."

"Maybe she just wants to know where it's all going to lead . . . you know, five, ten years down the road," I said.

"Hell, boy, we've lasted fifteen already, it's not like one of your teenage puppy-dog affairs where everybody dissolves like soggy Froot Loops every time someone gets a new pimple." I was not exactly swimming chin-deep in "teenage puppy-dog affairs" at the time, but I decided to let that pass. I think I got the point.

Dad stomped off into the trailer to pack his gear, while I went over to Gram's pickup and threw Dad's Everlasts in the back. We always had to count on using Gram's old Dodge every time Mom took off with Vanessa in the Chevy. Gram got the truck secondhand from a pig farmer. Painted it a different color every year just to be fashionable. She could always claim it as a business expense, as long as Gate o' Palms was stenciled in across the door. The only thing that stayed the same was the red-and-white peppermint stripes on the roll bar, which Gram thought enhanced the trade-in value because it was so irresistible.

I gunned the engine a couple of shots, and Dad came tearing out across the drive with his coveralls unzipped all the way down to no-man's-land. I could see that he was already wearing his good-luck passion-pink wrestling trunks. He had a towel tucked in around the collar just like a heavyweight boxer, and you'd have thought he was ready to take on Gorilla Monsoon and the Graham Brothers in a best-two-out-of-three, no-time-limit grudge match for the undisputed right to wear the championship belt of the world.

Dad slid into the cab beside me and snapped the door shut. "Let her hum, Half Nelson, old buddy. We gonna show the old General a few of our tricks." And he gave me a big thwack on the thigh right through my jeans. I knew he was floating sky-high inside and ready to beat the world just one more time; somewhere down inside me I got a glow of my own that I knew was more than just the hot stinging in my leg. Maybe it would be all right, I thought, maybe this would be the big time, and Mom would have to see it could work.

And so I thrummed that old Dodge right out the Gate o' Palms driveway onto the highway, leaving a spray of gravel to scatter in my wake. Jungle Fever was twelve miles down and over, and we were on our way.

"I sure hope they got some good insurance down there," I yelled over the sound of the highway and the wind gushing through the cab, " 'cause they're gonna have their hands full of trouble when the Gator Man starts comin' on the prowl."

20

5

*Oooh ooooh ohooooh oooooh oooooooh aaaaah aaaaahhh
aaaaaahhh   oooooooohhhhhh   oooooooooohhhhhh
ooooooohhhhh   KAAAAAAAWWWWW   KKKKAAAA
KKKKKAWWWWWWWW.* The old General had his sound
system cranked up full tilt, and it sounded like he was
playing the sound track from every Tarzan movie ever made.
Even from out on the highway you could catch the classic
jungle symphony in two movements. Part one was the restless jungle noise, where all the monkeys start to screech
and howl, then the birds shriek and you can hear their
wings flutter and beat, and then the monkeys pick it up
again in unison like a whole church full of demented boy
sopranos. Part two is the heavy artillery, usually ending
with the famous "Great Jungle Beasts to the Rescue" over-
ture. The star performers here are a few surly lions growling
sideways, sounding like raspy jets passing overhead. And

21

of course the big finale is the trumpeting elephants, plenty eager to come stampeding to the rescue.

We were just parking the truck when we heard the flip side come on. It was the equally famous jungle-drum routine, only there was a scratch in the record, and so the primitive pulsating jungle rhythm sounded more like a giant cricket. By the time we got up to the ticket booth, I guess we were ready to be ambushed by Pygmies. Well, I was half right. The General himself lunged right out from behind the ticket counter, still dressed like the great white hunter.

"Well, good morning, Johnny . . . er, excuse me, Gator Man—isn't that right, sonny?" And he gives me this heavy-duty cornball wink that puckers up the entire side of his face. I figure I'll straighten him out about the "sonny" stuff later, but right now I'm trying to slide my way out from under his slightly slimy arm, which he has draped around me just like one of those billboard pythons.

"Let's us have a little chitchat in my office. You can change in there, Gator, and maybe the boy can have a little sody pop," the General said, steering us into this jungle lean-to slapped together out of plastic bulrushes.

"We call the boy Nelson, Mr. Lee," my dad said in his most respectful tone.

"Yes . . . Nelson—that's a right fine name for a young man," the General said, like he'd just discovered sincerity. I was trying to think happy thoughts about the General, but it was hard. The best I could do right then was when I decided he looked more like some guy out of a cartoon than a real person. His little hunter outfit helped, I suppose, the way his melon gut pushed against his shirt, straining at the buttons until you got hypnotized just watching for them to pop. Then out of this little moon-pie bottom swathed in shorts came these two legs skinny as garden hoses. From the neck down, he was mostly Mr. Magoo. From the neck up he was more of a gerbil.

Anyhow, when we get into the office, the first thing I notice is the walls plastered with a thousand or so glossy photos, all the same identical 99¢ Kmart specials. I kind of shuffle up to one wall and notice that most of them are pictures of the General with all these greats and not-so-greats. Everyone has a little message written across the bottom to prove that the General really knew these guys. Here are a few of them, as near as I can remember.

To a finger-lickin' good guy—Col. Harland Sanders
In this one they both have on white Stetsons and string ties.

To my good buddy the General. Best always—Buffalo Bob
Buffalo Bob is a guy with a lot of fringe on his jacket. He and the General are sitting on stools, and the General has a puppet in his lap that's supposed to be Howdy Doody. The General has this look like Howdy just wet the General's pants.

FLIPPER
There the General is standing on a diving board and holding out this mackerel while Flipper is about halfway up to the fish. Flipper, by the way, was probably the most famous porpoise that ever lived, although he might have been a dolphin.

Good Luck to a chump from the Champ—Muhammad Ali
In this one Ali is faking getting hit, with his neck snapped to the side, while the General has his fist just ticking the champ's chin. The fist looks like a small potato.

From what I could see, the rest of the pictures were pretty much the same idea. The General had at one time or another managed to wangle pictures from Ronald McDonald, Phyllis Diller, Pete Rose, a family of midgets, Howard Cosell, Jerry Lewis, Denny Terco, Meadowlark Lemon, Dr. Joyce Brothers, Jimmy the Greek, Arturo the Human Cannonball, George Corley Wallace, Haystack Calhoun, Gentle Ben, Indio the Human Pincushion, Little Jimmy Dickens, Grizzly Adams, Joe Garagiola, Angelo Dundee and half the Solid Gold Dancers. It was pretty obvious from all that that the General either knew a lot of famous people or was the biggest groupie to ever come down the Florida Turnpike.

I was still gaping at the celebrity luminaries when the General taps me on the back of the neck with a cold bottle of Diet Truade. "Try this, Nelson," he says. "Hope you like it. It's all I ever drink. Your father's changing in the john; he'll be right out."

"No problem. Hey, where'd you get all these pictures?"

"You know what, Nelson, a lot of folks ask me that all the time. People, I always tell them. Work forty years with people, and if God chooses to bless you, He fills your life with many rewards. My reward has been to rub elbows with some of the giants of our industry, and those are just a few of them you see up there on the walls."

"Our industry?" I give him my puzzled look and take a hit of my Truade. Seems I'd heard that speech on something like the Merv Griffin show, only it wasn't the General who gave it.

"It's a family, really, Nelson. Industry sounds too much like a machine. The family of joy-givers, the mirth-makers, the special people who share of themselves and their gifts in bringing laughter to the millions."

24

Now I was positive I'd heard this before. "You in show business, something like that?" I tried again.

"Have you ever heard of the Ringlings, John Ringling North, and even further back, Mr. Phineas T. Barnum?" I nodded. "Great showmen, Nelson, legends, no more like them. I was hardly older than you are now when I decided that would be my life, too. I've been with some of the big ones, given my life to that vision, and I've been at it one way or another for an awful lot of years. I think your dad has that magic, too, Nelson. And I want to help him use it."

The General had started pacing back and forth and talking real loud like he was in some trial movie and this was the summing-up. I'm certain the Gator Man was catching all this through the bathroom door. I had just drained the last of the Truade, and for some reason was thinking back to what Mom had said about the dancing chicken, when suddenly the Gator Man pokes his head out the bathroom door like a nervous bride checking to see if the sheets have been turned down.

"Give us a peek, Johnny boy, no time to be shy," the General calls out. My dad slips back into the bathroom and closes the door.

"I AIN'T NO SIDESHOW FREAK, JUST YOU REMEMBER THAT UP FRONT, 'CAUSE THIS IS THE LAST DAMN TIME YOU'LL EVER CATCH JOHN ANTHONY GATO IN ANY GOON-SHOW RIG LIKE THIS!" Dad bellows this from behind the closed door. From what he says, I expect him to come toe-dancing out in leotards wearing a sequin hairnet and a tutu. But instead, when he finally gets pumped up enough, he just sort of lunges out the door. He stands there with his hands on his hips like he'd just graduated from the Jolly Green Giant School of Modeling. He's wearing some suit the General

25

must have had packed in mothballs since P. T. Barnum's last going-out-of-business sale. It was nothing more than the classic old-timey strongman's suit, all leopard-spotted and a one-strapper, slung over the right shoulder. If my dad could have sprouted a huge handlebar mustache right then and there, he might have actually passed for a genuine circus version of the world's strongest man. Unfortunately, this was the twentieth century, and so instead my dad looked more like a bad joke out of the back of some antique comic book.

"So what am I supposed to do? Bend steel bars with my teeth? Bite the heads off chickens? Pick up an elephant by its tail, or chew glass and swallow some tenpenny nails for dessert?" I could see that he was hurt and a little embarrassed about all this—and so he decided to get angry before the General caught on to how he really felt.

"Johnny, you're absolutely gorgeous. Relax." The General was fingering his mustache, half hiding a little smile. "Consider this phase one in your new career. Today you're going to learn the first lesson of every good showman—presence. You've got to give the people a show, make them know you're someone special. Whether you're a lion tamer or an opera star, the people want to *believe* you. Even a wrestler—look at the great ones, Gorgeous George to Ivan Putzky, they can all make that audience groan and cheer and swear and sweat bullets. You'll do that, too, someday, Johnny, but it takes work, lots of it."

"So what's for beginners?" my dad asks.

"Three days ago you did a brave thing, saving your daughter from a pit of gators. Today you become the Gator Man for good. You go up against a gen-you-wine man-eating gator, one-on-one, no holds barred. Actually, it's just a tired old cow gator at the end of the line—but no one has to know that. And *you* are going to make those fine drooling people out there believe, really *believe*, that it's life or death."

"You mean I'm going to fake it?" Dad was getting that look on his face like the time he ate the rotten cashews. "So that's the big exhibition—no wrestling with a legitimate opponent, just a lot of rolling around with a sick alligator?"

"Sort of," the General answers. "And make it . . . convincing. A lot of noise, grunts. The folks like noise. Stretch it out a bit, give the old cow a few moments, you know, like it's hanging in the balance. Then when you think everyone's gotten their money's worth, you take the old gator down for the last time. Just roll her over, give her a few strokes on the belly, and she's Play-dough. And bing, bing, you're on your way."

"And what about the TV matches? More alligators?" my dad asks.

"Getting those lined up . . . strictly on the level, against some comers, new blood. Just do good today, the other will come soon enough." The General finished with a tough-guy little spit on the floor for punctuation. Only nothing made it to the floor.

"Yeah, well, maybe let's let this be the first and last warm-up. I don't have much of a taste for mud. Okay, General?"

And the General, halfway out the door, calls back over his shoulder, "We'll just see. . . . Remember, Johnny, patience is a virtue. Just ask your boy about virtues. He's a good boy."

And Dad steers me out the door behind the General, holding me by the scruff of the neck. He gives me a little squeeze. Which means that just between him and me he knows better, and it's gonna be all right.

6

"Is that your old man, Nelson? God, that's really rank." I could smell Heidi Tedesco before I even turned to see her standing at my side. It was the same Tigress Desire cologne that she used to pollute Room 38 all last year when she sat beside me in "Our Government Today," combing out tangles throughout most of the legislative process right up to the pocket veto. She was sort of founding queen mother of the teenage drones, a bunch of cut-rate scumbags who hung around shopping centers and lifted magazines from Wilson's Drugs. Their biggest contribution at school was setting fire to the towel dispensers, which is why you've got to drip dry now if you're courageous enough to wash your hands in the basement in the first place.

"Yeah, well what if it is my old man? So what's your father, a brain surgeon?" I popped back at her.

"No, my old man's a dork. Least, Mom says so. He took

off for Michigan six years ago with some woman who grooms poodles. Mom says if they ever show up around here again she's going to tie pink ribbons to their tails and call the dogcatcher." Heidi put her foot up on the two-by-four that made a rough fence around the General's makeshift wrestling ring. She slung her elbow across her knee and studied the action, like she was some big-league pitching coach watching from the dugout. "How come he don't get chewed up doing that?" she asked.

I tried my best to explain the techniques of gator wrestling, maybe making it sound a little more hazardous than it really was. My dad was standing at his full height, sort of holding the wasted old gator across his chest, and then with a big theatrical *unnnnhhh* flipped the gator up into the air and fell flat backward onto the canvas under the gator like he had been thrown down for the pin. It was very convincing, and Heidi practically bolted into the ring when she saw my dad flailing about on the canvas like a beached whale.

"Get up and handle that sucker, handle 'im!" she yelled. The rest of the crowd was caught up in the action, too, pelting that gator with mashed-in popcorn boxes and screaming for my dad to get up. The more they screamed, the more Dad just lay there, shaking out the cobwebs like he was coming out of a Ripple hangover. The old dazed-and-confused routine was always surefire to get the folks roaring. Across the ring I could see the General sitting ringside on a folding campstool, stroking the knob top of a palm-cane walking stick. He looked like a Cheshire cat with a bellyful of canaries. Dad must have been passing his audition.

"Tell him to get up, for cripes' sake, tell him, you Nelson, tell your old man to get off his fat ass and do something,"

Heidi screamed in my ear. She hooked me by an elbow and was dragging me toward the ring. In her free hand she was juggling a grape sno-cone, holding it aloft like a torch and flailing it around in a wild attempt at keeping her balance. She could have passed for a nuthouse Statue of Liberty impersonator. She had me practically up to the two-by-four fence and had started over it to the ring when I decided to reclaim my elbow.

But I must have pulled back a little too fast. When her foot caught on the two-by-four she did a modified backward belly whopper into the crowd along the fence and landed facedown in this Mormon-looking family of tourists. Now, there's some fundamental principle of physical science at work here, because the equal and opposite reaction of her falling into the crowd was when the grape-soaked clump of ice from her sno-cone, frozen into a perfect ball, lofted its way out of the Dixie paper cone Heidi was clutching and landed center ring like some bombadier's dream—*schwop*—dead center onto my father's chest. A purple stain, almost as bright as the red in my father's face, spread across the leopard leotards.

The crowd was loving it when my dad went into his Gator Man rage, only they didn't know that it was for real. I could tell by the way his jaw locked and his eyes glassed up that it wasn't the kiddie hour anymore. After waltzing with a burned-out gator, he must have figured that a sno-cone to the breastbone was really scraping bottom, careerwise. He grabbed the helpless gator by the tail and ran it around the ring like a vacuum cleaner. Then he held it overhead and body-slammed it to the canvas, and again, two more times.

The gator was about ready to check out, but my dad just reared one leg and let fly with the most deadly knee drop I'd ever seen him put to anyone. There was a ferocious, sickening *crack* like an old tree limb giving way, and the gator shivered and then went perfectly still—for good.

My dad bounded out of the ring and plowed his way right through the crowd. Some little kids let go with a few whistles and squeaky little cheers, but they were muffled out pretty fast by their assorted mothers. Otherwise there wasn't a sound. The crowd dissolved into separate lumps of people and drifted off in all directions, leaving only the General sitting across the ring with his hands crossed over his cane, concentrating like he was planning the Invasion of Normandy. And in the ring center a family of flies buzzed in tight spirals and then came to rest on the horny ridges above the gator's staring eyes.

I am just about to the main gate, heading for the parking lot to wait for my dad to show up, when Heidi swoops down on me like a hungry pelican. She had obviously been hiding out with the jungle birds, for she was holding a bouquet of ratty-looking ostrich feathers. A long curving purple plume stuck in her hair, Pocahontas-style. "What a freak! Honest to God, Nelson, he should have his own cage right here," she said.

"Yeah, and yours should be right next to his. What were you trying to prove by going into the ring? You've really got some first-class brains. You and your damn sno-cone," I said, trying to walk away.

"Well, if it hadn't been for that sno-cone, your father would look like a pile of fish bait by now. Besides, you're the one that practically ripped my arm off. Here, stick these in your tail and fly away," she said, throwing her handful of feathers in my face.

She was still right behind me as I got to the pickup. "That gator was an antique, and my father knew what he was doing. Only thing you accomplished was flipping out my

31

dad and getting that gator killed. Why don't you go steal some more perfume, or work on your stamp collection, whatever you do in your spare time."

"Maybe I'll just follow you and your old man around all summer. I can pick up all your leftovers and open a gator-skin handbag shop in Sarasota. Nice truck," she said, stroking the tailgate like it was made of mink. "Yours? How about a ride?"

"My grandmother's," I answered. "Where you going? You live up by the bypass? We're at the Gate o' Palms."

"Close enough," she said, hopping in the back. "I can always hitch from there if my old lady's not home." She hunkered down with her back against the cab and sat cross-legged with a hand on each knee. Her mouth went into this pout, like she wasn't so sure if she was a nuisance. Neither was I.

I jumped up into the truck bed and sat along the side with my arm draped over the tire well. I watched Heidi scrunching up sand in her toes. She was a lean brown girl with one of those perpetual coffee tans that seems totally unrelated to anything having to do with the sun. Her jeans were too tight, and she seemed to have a lifetime supply of bare-middle tops so she could flash her belly button like the headlight on a locomotive. Her hair was thick and black— sometimes when she braided it with little gold chains you could have sworn she just barged in from the Fertile Crescent. But with her Tigress cologne and her watermelon bubble gum there were some days you had to have terminal sinus congestion just to get near her. She did all the makeup numbers, too—raccoon mascara eyes and twenty-eight shades of lipstick, usually the glossy iridescent stuff that looks like the frosting on a turnover. And nails to match, shimmering like glazed shells. Even with her toes scuffling in the dirt

of Gram's truck, her toenails looked like those little co-
quinas that bury themselves in the wet sand along Manatee
Beach after every high tide.

"Wanna take a picture?" She had caught me staring at
her toes.

"Sorry."

"Mom gets nail polish at cost in her store. All the latest
shades. And I get her leftovers." She held her toes up and
wiggled them like the polish was still drying.

"Your mom's got a store?" I asked.

"Nah, just works in one. Roberta's House of Beauty.
Roberta is actually a guy."

"What's his name? Robert, and he added an *a*?"

"No, Mel Furnier. Roberta's his cat."

"Then it's really the cat's store?"

"I think the cat's dead." And so's your brain, I was going
to say until I saw my dad come walking in slow, scuffling
steps across the lot to the truck. He had the truck keys in
his right hand, and he kept his eyes fixed on them like they
were the only thing safe enough to look at. His Everlasts
were laced together and wrapped around his neck, where
they stayed even after he entered the cab and started the
engine. I stayed in back, not so much to keep Heidi company as to give my dad some time to sort of settle into
himself. I knew he probably felt as low-down miserable as
could be. Once news of the big Jungle Fever Massacre
reached home, the Gate o' Palms would become a National
Historical Landmark, like Harpers Ferry, the Concord
Bridge, Little Big Horn and Dealy Plaza all rolled into one.

7

It was raining the next morning and, like the weathermen say, there would be more of the same all day long. It was a big Gulf of Mexico thunderclapper, and you could hear it rumbling toward you for almost an hour before dawn, when the rains finally showed up. I was up by six-thirty. The rain slanted down from the west, rattling against the trailers.

The paper kid had forgotten to wrap the *Morning Courier* in one of those waterproof plastic sheaths. It was ready to dissolve into wood pulp and printer's ink when I rescued it from the front steps. I unfolded it and separated the sections and popped it in the oven at low heat for thirty minutes. After the trailer filled up with the smell of crisp, fresh-baked newsprint, I pulled the paper out and spread it across the breakfast bar. The front section was the usual doomsday trash: price hikes, wage freezes, union walkouts

34

and Today's Chuckle. But the real chuckle was on page one, section two. GATOR DIES IN TRAGIC STUNT. It didn't get much better when you got down to small print:

PALMETTO, July 11. A promotion "exhibition" intended to highlight the opening of Jungle Fever, a Palmetto area animal ranch attraction, ended tragically today with the death of a female alligator.

The gator died as a result of injuries sustained in a "wrestling match" with John Anthony Gato, billed as the "Gator Man." Gato, a local resident with previous professional wrestling experience, was reported by eyewitnesses to have gone somewhat berserk at the end of the match.

An autopsy done at the request of the ASPCA and the Florida Sheriff's Department indicated severe spinal damage. One observer described the incident as a "brutal display" in which the animal was repeatedly slammed to the canvas.

A spokesman for the Sheriff's Department said the incident is under investigation. The ASPCA has launched its own private investigation into the matter.

A state statute protecting the alligator could serve as a basis of prosecution in this case. The State Attorney General's Office could not be reached for comment.

Newspapers. They missed so much—the sno-cone, the leopardskin tights, the things going on inside John Anthony Gato. They didn't know about Mom or Vanessa or me, or even Heidi Tedesco, and they sure didn't know about how hard people have to try sometimes and what they have to give up along the way. And they didn't know about my Aunt Ruthie in Georgia, or about all the weeds in Gate o' Palms, which Dad and I pulled out on our hands and knees, one by one by one.

The night before had been quiet. Dad had walked out the county road, probably to the end. He got back at midnight, even after Mom had made it back from the Groveland Drive-in. She had taken Vanessa to a Wilderness Family double feature. Vanessa just ate up all that log-cabin-togetherness stuff.

Suddenly the toilet flushed—reveille. Mom came gliding into the kitchen knotting the belt around her green chenille robe, like she was tying a tourniquet.

"You're bright and early Nelson. What's the occasion?" she asked. She went to the sink and stared at last night's dishes. Her face curdled like she smelled something dead.

"No occasion, just the rain," I answered. "Dried the paper out." I folded it up and chucked it onto the breakfast bar. It slid off and fell over the side.

"Was the Gator Man a big hit at the zoo? Did he win a teddy bear?" The sink was filling with scalding water. Mom took off her rings and poured in some soap and sudsed it up with her hand. I could see the purple blots on the backs of her legs where the veins had exploded under the skin. She said she didn't need some doctor to tell her she had waitress legs.

"It's really more of a jungle animal ranch than a zoo, Mom," I corrected. I decided then that I would have to be the one to tell her. Dad wasn't a coward, but maybe I could soften things by getting there first. "It all went haywire,

36

Mom. Started off fine, but then something happened. I think he felt jerky at first in this jungle-man getup the General made him wear. But things settled down and would have been okay if the crowd hadn't of gone crazy." Why was I avoiding Heidi's moronic grandstand play? "Anyhow, Dad was kinda getting pelted with stuff, and I guess he took it out on the gator. By accident. Was all a mistake. I know Dad probably wishes he could just . . . dissolve or something." Mom stood stock-still at the sink. I was dreading seeing her look when she turned around, but she didn't. Just stood there with her hands hanging limp in the hot water.

"The paper made it sound so cold-blooded. . . . Pure newspaper bullshit," I continued.

"Oh, Nelson . . . He's in the paper? . . . The newsper? . . . Oh, God preserve us. Where is it?"

I picked the paper off the floor where it had fallen and laid it on the counter beside the sink. Mom read the story, half mumbling the words to herself, repeating certain parts. Not once did she touch the newspaper. When she was finished she went back to washing the dishes without saying a word. After the dishes were stacked in the strainer, Mom drained the sink and stood silently staring into the empty basin. A series of almost invisible shudders rippled across her back, twitching into her shoulders. Her head bobbed a couple of times and then she swallowed hard.

"Do me a favor, Nelson, hon," she finally said. "Go into your room and pull all of Vanessa's clothes out of her dresser. Take them out and put them in the trunk of the car. Try not to get them too wet."

"No," I said, and knew instantly it was the wrong response.

"No what?" Mom snapped. She stood against the sink, drying her hands on the hem of her nightgown and daring me to go on.

"No, don't go. No, don't run off with Vanessa, not now, not when we need . . ."

"Need *me*? Need, that's a good one, Nelson. Your needing days are just about over. And him, your so-called father— all he needs is a straitjacket. Now get going."

It took me two trips to get all of Vanessa's stuff. When I came back into the kitchen the second time, Mom had piles of her own things on the floor. She stuffed all her underwear into one shopping bag and all the shoes that would fit into another. She took two armfuls of clothes, still on hangers, out to the car and threw them full-length across the backseat.

"Now Vanessa," she whispered to me. "Try not to wake her up." I went into our room and slid my arms under Vanessa where she slept in the bottom bed of our old ranch-house bunk combination from Sears. It was the only bed we had ever had. She stirred some, but I covered her head and wrapped her around completely in her spread. It was a short run to the car, so I was able to avoid getting her soaked in the blowing rain. I nestled her sideways on the front seat and pulled the spread back from her head so she could breathe a little more easily. I wanted to wake her up and try to explain things to her, but it might be years before she could really understand, if she ever did. Right then, she just looked like one of those refugee children you're always seeing on the news, wrapped in frizzled blankets drinking powdered milk out of a wooden bowl. She would adjust, I figured. Little kids can handle just about anything.

But me, inside I was frantic, spinning around, looking for a place to land. Mom, Dad, Vanessa. Whose side was

I on? Why did there have to be sides anyway? We had never had anything much but each other, and now we were losing that too.

When I got back into the kitchen, Mom had dressed and was stuffing everything from the medicine cabinet into a plastic bag from C'est Chic Boutique. She pulled the drawstring tight, making what looked like a lumpy punching bag.

"There," she declared to herself, "that'll do us till we get settled. Just tell your father we had to go. Tell him we hope this mess blows over and things work out, this bit in the newspaper, I mean. You take care, Nelson, and watch over him. Vanessa still needs a mother, but there's not much more you need from me." She reached out her arm with the bag. I thought she was handing it to me, but instead she pulled me over and put a big smothering bear hug on me.

"Are you guys going for keeps?" I asked. My voice sounded strange.

"I don't know, maybe . . . probably."

"Aunt Ruthie's? Does she know?"

"I told Ruthie we might be up. I don't think she'll be surprised. I'll send you a note sometime after we're settled. Probably not right away."

"We can still get together sometime, can't we?" I asked, each word squeezing out through the thickening lump in my throat.

"Maybe," she answered, but not very convincingly. She loosened our embrace and held me at arm's length by the shoulders. "And get rid of that nickname . . . Half Nelson, that's a dumb joke. You're almost, well, a man now. Tell your father it doesn't fit you anymore. Promise me."

"All right." I nodded.

39

"And pay the phone bill. I left the money by the toaster. We're two months overdue, and they'll cut us—you—off if it's not paid. You're gonna run things around here from now on. Here's a kiss from Vanessa. Now 'bye." She gave me a little smooch on the cheek and then slipped out the door holding the bag over her head against the rain. She never did believe in raincoats.

The old Chevy coughed and spit but finally turned over and took off, gurgling like it was underwater. The tailpipe still dangled from the rear. They'd be lucky to make it to Georgia, but then Mom never pushed it, and Vanessa would have to stop to pee every twenty minutes. The storm had gotten its second wind. It was coming in squalls and gusts, with clots of thick rain swirling across the ground. Once under way, the Chevy drove under the straining palm arch and out onto the highway, turning left, northbound, and disappeared into the gray morning.

8

When I got down to the police station three days later, my dad was stripped to the waist and handcuffed to an old steam radiator.

"Is that man over there your father?" the sergeant asked me. I looked at him and he looked away.

"Yes, sir," I answered.

"You don't have to call that *basketass cop* 'sir,' Nelson."

"Yes, sir, that's him," I repeated, trying to ignore my dad. "What's going on? Where'd you find him?"

After Mom and Vanessa took off, Dad acted like it was perfectly natural, them going and all. He spent the rest of that morning glued to the tube, from "Good Morning America" right up to the noontime newsbreak. After lunch he threw his and mom's bed, mattress and all, out on the lawn and set it on fire. He doused it with enough Charcoal lighter fluid for a Texas barbecue, lit it all over with a newspaper torch, and watched it burn until the fluid was used up and the rain doused it out. It mostly singed the mattress and left a big burned rectangle on the grass. Then he went back in and tied all the drapes in knots, screaming, "Pussy curtains, pussy curtains" at the top of his lungs. That's when I cleared out for Gram's.

We watched for an hour, expecting the trailer to blow up. But nothing happened. I was ready to sneak back over there to check for bodies or something when Dad tears out of the door wearing the only suit he's ever owned in his entire life. He called it his bouncer costume, but it was just a three-piece Palm Beach special, Havana weave and tropical green. The other noteworthy difference was that his head was shaved, perfectly smooth and oyster white.

He was heading for Gram's truck, and I tore off after him. I wanted to settle him down before he ended up as Teddy Delgado's bunkmate in Chattahoochee. I caught up with him and tried to grab him by the arm. He gave me a forearm shiver, hopped in the truck and was gone. I figured he was heading off after Mom and Vanessa, and they'd all be back home in a couple of days, fussing and scrapping just like old times. I was just about ready for them to roll in when I got the call from police headquarters.

"We got him for DWI, driving to endanger, breaking and entering, vandalism and aggravated assault. It's a mighty big ticket, boy," the sergeant said, "and that's not to mention that other mess with that gator, which is something we're still looking into."

"So what's that all mean? Is he going to jail?" I'd seen enough of those cop shows to know that you had to get things explained; otherwise you'd be doing hard time before the previews came on for next week's episode.

"Seems your daddy went on a little rampage," the cop

explained. "Got himself juiced up on bad medicine and did some damage. Smeared some hot blacktop goop over all those Jungle Fever signs up and down the state. Took the state police on a real fox hunt. Then he came back here and tore loose on the park itself. This General Lee fellow called us hisself—'bout four-thirty last night. A break-in. Seems your daddy raised hell down there, let the monkeys out, chased half the birds away, messed over some of the cages real bad. Was heading for his gator friends when the General caught up to him. Came upside the General's head, like to break his jaw. Tore loose on that little jungle hut like it was shredded wheat. That's when we showed up— looked like a hurricane hit out there. Hell, boy, we're still rounding up flamingos far out as Mullet Key."

"Why in the name of God would you do a thing like that, Daddy?" I asked, walking over to where he sat now, with his back against the radiator and his one arm dangling above his head from the handcuff. He looked like one of those cartoon dungeon dwellers, minus the full-length beard.

"Because that little two-dollar fart hasn't got no right keeping all those little creatures in bondage. I was gonna liberate all of 'em, back to where they came from. It's an act against nature, is all; it shouldn't be allowed."

"Dad, these guys are going to lock you up. Did you ever stop to think that Mom might not want to come back to some convict?"

"Oh, bullhunkers, Nelson, she ain't never gonna come back anyways. She's been itching for a reason to haul tail ever since she figured I wasn't never gonna make Father of the Year or own a chain of car washes. Must think she can do better somewheres else, and maybe she's right. It don't bother me none, neither. Goodspeed and more power to her."

"Godspeed," I corrected. Dad's command of speech fizzled sometimes when his feathers got ruffled.

"Godspeed, goodspeed, full speed ahead and damn the torpedoes, we used to say. It's over is all I'm sayin'. They can put me on a friggin' chain gang and I'll cut cane from here to Key West and back again. I'll be a damn fine convict, and if anyone wants trouble, I can kick ass till from now to Judgment Day."

I swear he was delirious. His huge chest throbbed and his mouth hung open, spit-soaked, sucking wind like he was breathing underwater. His face had a three days' stubble and his glistening head gave him a gray look, like some old wino at death's door. He collapsed back, wilting against the radiator. He was really beaten for the first time, I thought. He'd been pounded right into the ground, all used up and ready to cash it in for good.

I think that must have been the absolute first time that I'd ever seen my dad give in. He'd been beaten down just about every way there was. That's about when I decided I had to figure some way to bring my dad back to the living. Only problem was, just then I didn't quite know how to even begin. Me and Dad could talk about practically anything—fishing for pompano and teenage social diseases and customizing vans and how to do isometrics in study hall and how to make chili pie and where to gig for the fattest frogs. But I'd never give my dad advice, and he didn't like pep talks. Words, he'd say, don't change nothin'. Then he'd snort and sniffle and walk away, hitching up his pants with his thumbs through the belt loops. Think Mom got the same routine. "Couldn't tell that man his nose was on fire," she used to say. But he could understand actions, most of all when they blasted him right between the eyeballs. Which is probably why Mom finally did her farewell thing once and for all.

So for sure I'd have to figure some really desperate scheme to smack Dad right square in the gut. If I was some eight-year-old runny-nosed wimp, I'd have probably held my breath or run away to the nearest Burger Paradise and scarfed down double-cheese combos until the police showed up. But we were in the majors now, twice that age and prime high school material. Time to exercise the developing intellect, to round up all the wit, cunning and plain old street smarts that I could manage. Only right then I couldn't manage much. It would have to come in good time, when my brain was all primed up. For now, it was enough to just figure how to keep my dad off the rock pile.

He was still raving himself into a terminal conniption fit when suddenly in walks the General. The big freeze comes over my dad, and he goes into a trance. "Right this way, Mr. Lee," the sergeant purrs, snapping right to attention. The two of them whizz right by us without even a sideways glance. They enter the chief's office the far corner of the room and close the door behind them. After about two minutes, the sergeant comes out and fetches a cone of water from the bottle cooler beside the door. It's still belching up bubbles when he disappears inside again.

"Pinhead cops," Dad grumbled. "Gonna let that pint o' piss screw me right to the wall. You just watch."

"Ease off, Dad. Probably just routine junk. Filing a complaint, you know."

"I'll give them a complaint. Look, Nelson, I want you to know that I'm . . . I'll make it. I don't want you to be sorry about me . . . all this mess. We'll straighten it out, we'll figure a way."

"Yeah, I think things'll come around." I sat down next to him with my back against the radiator. Right then, I felt that it would be easier to rehabilitate the Hillside Strangler. I could have gotten sick, I was turning around inside so fast. "Let's just see what they want to do with us." The "us" part just slipped in there unexpected. Suddenly it seemed that me and Dad were costarring in some cheapie drive-in movie—we were the last two surviving humans, locked up together while an alien race decided our fate. I was hoping they weren't going to dissect us.

"May we talk without having to restrain you, Mr. Gato?" The captain had come out of his office first, followed by General Lee and the sergeant. He stood over us, thumping a rolled-up bundle of papers against his thigh. Dad nodded without lifting his head.

"The handcuffs, sergeant," the captain ordered, and the sergeant produced a key and unlocked my dad's hands from the radiator. Dad flexed the arm for a moment and then pulled himself up to his full height.

"Go on ahead. Let's hear it," Dad said.

"Over here," the captain said, indicating the sergeant's desk. They all sat while I hung back by the radiator.

"First of all, Mr. Gato," the captain began, "I should explain that we are not obligated by law to make deals, or horse-trade, if you will. However, the General has advised us of some exceptional circumstances that we feel might be extenuating in this instance." The captain shot me a quick look. He must have known about Mom and Vanessa.

"Quite simply, Mr. Gato, the General is willing to drop all charges arising out of your, uh, misconduct at his establishment last night. Yet he feels you are obligated to make some restitution."

"Pay him back? Sorry," Dad said. "I'm down to spare change already."

"Well, actually, the General has more in mind of a work situation. Restore some of the damaged items, ah, provide a little muscle, maintenance, that sort of thing. You and the General would, of course, work out the specific terms of the agreement. I understand he had a standing deal with you already for some wrestling matches. That could be figured into the terms of the arrangement."

"Well, I think that was just bait, if you know what I mean, captain," Dad said.

"Mouthwash, pure and simple," the General exploded.

"Now, gentlemen, let's keep it nice and friendly," said the captain. "Of course there are still some other loose ends. . . . The state police might have to be dealt with about those driving charges. And there's still that matter of the gator that people are all puffed up about. But nothing insurmountable by a long shot. Small potatoes, comparatively speaking. So what do you say?"

My dad sat twisting at his knuckles, fidgeting. It was a good offer on the surface, but it sounded to me like that indentured servant stuff, where somebody owns you till you've worked your way to freedom. Everything that was wrong already seemed to have started at Jungle Fever in the first place. We were getting deeper and deeper, stuck in with the General just like he was the tar baby. The more you fought it, the more you got sucked in.

"How about it, Half Nelson? Whadda we tell the captain here?" Dad turned in his seat and looked me dead on in the eyes. He wasn't just humoring his little Half Nelson anymore, neither. I could tell from the blank way that he

47

looked at me that he really needed an answer.

"It's all kinda sudden like," I answer. "Why don't we take a weekend to think it through?"

"Can we do that?" asked my dad, turning back to the captain.

"Fair enough. I suppose we can. We'll release you on your own recognizance, which means you got to stick close at home. And no more crazy stuff. We'll need to hear your answer by nine o'clock Monday morning. Otherwise we go on with the charges. So take the time to think it over, maybe talk to a lawyer. We'll be in touch."

And they all stood at once like the "Star-Spangled Banner" was playing somewhere in their heads. The General did a little pirouette and waddled right past me. I could see a swelling under his right ear down along the jaw, sort of gray and green like rotten onions. Dad must have caught him a good one. The sergeant and the captain whispered together for a few seconds, and then the captain wagged a scolding finger, thick as a breakfast sausage, right in my dad's face. He must have been kidding, because he still had his finger when my dad turned to leave.

"Let's go, Half Nelson," Dad said, brushing my hair to one side, like Mom used to when I was little. I could deal with that; things were different now. "I guess this means I'm in your custody. Think you're up to it?"

"No harm trying," I said. "Guess that means I'll have to start shaping you up, get you on the old straight and narrow."

"It's high time somebody tried. Hope you're the man for the job."

"Yeah, me, too. Now let's get on home before somebody changes their mind."

9

And so Monday comes, and Dad doesn't even call the chief. He just shows up at Jungle Fever, eight sharp, with my old Jetsons lunch box full of bologna sandwiches. The General's face is back to normal-puffy, and he seems to be in a forgiving mood. They go off together to call the chief from the General's office, or what's left of it.

I locked the truck, making sure to leave the windows open a crack. It was getting to the miserable part of summer, when the roads get sticky hot and the old ladies carry parasols just to walk to their mailboxes. Best you could hope for was an afternoon thunderstorm, but even that was like spitting on the bottom of a hot iron. "No relief in sight" was how they said it on the radio. Everybody hung out in shopping malls or movies, air-conditioned comfort. "Come in, it's coooool inside" the sign would say, with a picture of a polar bear on these big drooping mounds of snow and ice. Or else they went to the beach. The tourists went to the Gulf, but anybody with half a brain went for the fresh water—rivers, sinkholes, lakes.

Lake Marjorie was my favorite. It was cheap and had pronto pups for 50¢ and a three-story tower where you could do cannonballs and break your eardrums if you hit at an angle. I hated to just take off and leave my dad to do the General's dirty work by himself, but I wanted to clear out and work on my plot to pull things together. Nothing clears the head like a good swim. Washes all the crap out. So I headed off for the lake, with my Converse all-star gym bag.

After about an hour of walking and hitching, I'm in the Lake Marjorie Bathhouse, slipping into my supersleek J.C. Penney surfbusters. It's still early, and the place is practically deserted. Perfect. I check in my basket of valuables and head for the water, dropping my towel on a plump little patch of sand. The water is still cold as iced tea, and about the same color. I walk in thigh deep, splash some water on my face and lunge on in like an icebreaker. *Cooooooooooosssssssshhhhhhhhhhhhh*. A total enema for the brain. I could defect to Russia and join the Polar Bear Club. It's thirty degrees below in Minsk and last one in's a rotten egg. *Cooooooooooosssssssshhhhhhhhhhhhh*.

Underwater for as long as my lungs can make it . . . gliding . . . 117 . . . 118 . . . 119 . . . 120 . . . push up to the sun and explode spray through my blowhole. Save the whales! Two minutes is no sweat. So dive again, gotta rip that harpoon out, take those killers for a ride. . . . I could relate to that whale stuff, let my arms wither into fins, and take off for the Antarctic.

I was getting deep. I opened my eyes . . . total blackness. The spring was nearby; I could feel the currents puls-

50

ing up over my legs, unraveling into the lake like giant ice-water serpents. My legs kicked, scissored, thrusting me down. I was going for the spring. The cold water thrummed against my forehead, flowed over me, chilling. My breath was almost gone; in seconds I could be breathing water into my lungs, filling them up like sponges. The brain would die, starving for oxygen. That would be the end of it, the end of Nelson Gato as we know him today.

It was such a perfect idea, foolproof, nothing like a death in the family to smooth out all the rough places. A good old-fashioned bit of tragedy, families pulling together, by-gones gone forever. Mom and Vanessa would have to find dresses. Decisions would be made: stones, inscriptions, a coffin of pine—or mahogany—a plot, someone to say a few words. "A fine son, a loving brother, a good citizen. . . . All those who knew young Nelson are diminished by this tragic and untimely blah blah blah. . . . The Lord is my shepherd. . . . We commit him into thy loving hands. . . ." There would be flowers and casseroles, and then all my T-shirts would go to Goodwill. And Mom and Dad would try it again, this time for the sake of Vanessa, their only surviving child, and for the memory of poor old unforgettable Nelson. An absolutely magnificent solution.

But maybe a touch drastic. I wasn't volunteering. Maybe I was being selfish, but what good was having everyone back together if I couldn't be around to enjoy it? And most of the good stuff was still ahead of me, like my own van and cruising the Bahamas, working on an oil platform and girls.

I hit surface, gasping and sputtering. Air! The back of my head throbbed like I'd just wolfed a gallon of ice cream. The diving tower stood over a hundred yards away, back toward shore. I had left the swimming area, lost my sense

51

of reckoning and gone well beyond everything into the black cold water that fed the lake. I rolled over on my back, drifting and stroking toward the tower, taking it easy. By the time I reached it, my breath had returned with my senses. I pulled myself up onto the first platform, and then climbed the ladder two more platforms up to the top. The wood was smoothed and bleached by years of water and sun. It held the morning's heat like flat stones warmed by a fire. I stretched out at full length, letting the heat bake right into my body. In another hour the sun would be approaching its full power. I turned over on my face and fell dead asleep.

10

"Touch me again and I'll scream, swear to God!" I turned
my head toward the voice and opened one eye just enough
to see Heidi skittering around the edge of the platform.
She was packed into this incredible bikini, made out of
something like tinfoil. It was Day-Glo orange, and tight as
a snare drum. The guy chasing her was right off a recruiting
poster—a dagger tatoo on his right bicep and curly blond
hair clipped right to his head along the sides, like white
sidewalls. He was edging Heidi onto the far corner of the
platform.

"That's close enough. Save it for later."

"Later, it's always later." The poster boy reached out and
grabbed Heidi around the waist. He pulled her tight against
him, grabbing everything he could, then slipped his hands
around back. He was trying to get under the Day-Glo tinfoil.

"I'm screaming, no lie. Get your paws off me, Dougie, no shit." Heidi was holding on to the guy to keep from falling and pushing him away at the same time.

"Leave her alone, pal," I say, standing up. I'm bigger than the guy, but he's solid. He turns, still holding on to Heidi by one wrist.

"Back off, sonny, or I'll break your ugly face," Dougie bellows, bracing his legs to hold his territory.

"Nelson Gato!" Heidi squeaks from behind this Dougie guy. "What are *you* doing up here?" Good question, I think, and I'm ready to start apologizing, like I just happened to be waiting for a bus to come along on the top platform in the middle of Lake Marjorie.

"You know this stootz, sugarcakes?" Figure it out—one minute he's groping her like a GI sex maniac, and the next minute it's sugarcakes.

"Sure I know him, he was in half my—we're practically buddies. I almost saved his old man's life."

"No foolin'," Dougie says. "Well, tell him we're havin' a discussion, and maybe he should take a nice dive and report to the kiddie pool. How about it, Nellie boy?"

"How about you try to make me?" I answered. Okay, so it was kinda corny, but I curled my lip a little when I said it, the maximum snotty comeback. Like any all-purpose playground dare, it put it all up to the other guy. In this case, I figured the only safe way to get Heidi away from this clone was to get him to come after me. Otherwise we'd all go off the high tower together—no telling how we'd get tangled up.

It worked. Dougie came right up into my face, breath-test close, and started jabbing in the breastbone with an index finger. That qualified as first contact, I figured, and so the next move was mine. I dropped down, grabbed one leg by the ankle and picked it up waist high, sweeping my right leg around from behind and knocking his other leg out from under. He had glommed onto my neck, but his grip broke when he fell—*crack*—right on his tailbone. A perfect one-leg takedown, right out of the textbook. It's lesson number one for any wrestler. But if you can execute, as Dad says, it's golden.

Dougie seemed to be reconsidering. I fell on top of him and pushed his face into the boards, grabbing an arm in a chicken wing. Lesson two: A chicken wing is what the TV cops do to a guy just before they stick a .38 into his eardrum and ask him where he stashed the girl, or the dope, or the money, or whatever they were stashing that particular week.

Dougie was wilting. Grinding facedown into the ragged boards seemed to cool him off. He kept whimpering something about getting splinters in his nose. I wasn't sure what I was going to do with him once I had him, but I kept applying little doses of leverage while I figured it out.

"Get out of here, Heidi," I yelled. "Jump, get to shore."

"You crazy?" was all she answered. She kept hugging herself like she had the chills.

Finally she walks to the ladder and starts down. Slowly. She's almost to the first platform, when she turns around and very carefully aims herself for a dive, hands together, arms above her head. One, two, three. I can see her pumping her arms, little practice strokes, and then *schwop*— still a belly-whopper! What a getaway.

I give Dougie my farewell speech: "Okay, now just cool down a little bit. I don't even know what this is all about— just don't go messin' over people, Heidi or anyone, understand?"

I let off on his arm and he rolled over, mumbling all kinds of filth under his breath. Guys like that are a little slow to catch on. Anyway, I figure he's not going to be too rowdy for a while.

"Give that arm a rest before you try swimming anywhere, unless you want to swim in circles. Good as new in no time." And then I went into my superhero exit, a blind dive right off the tower. Came down five feet away from this redheaded kid, practically totaled the poor little bastard. I took off stroking and gliding, and still managed to overtake Heidi about twenty feet from shore.

"Get your stuff. We're going," I ordered. Heidi was slogging through the waist-deep water, with me right in her wake.

"Where's Dougie?" she asked.

"Still on the tower. Who gives a damn?"

"He's gonna really be pissed." We were standing on the beach. The place was knee-deep by now in bodies, radios, Frisbees. I found my towel among the clutter of inflatable ducks, turtles, sea gulls, dragons and assorted Big Birds.

"Where's your things?"

"Tables," she said, twisting her head in the direction of the snack bar. Two rows of redwood picnic tables sat chained to each other, to discourage someone sneaking out with one hidden in his jockstrap.

Heidi slung a canvas bag over her shoulders and slipped a pair of sunglasses on top of her head. "Here, pick up Dougie's stuff. He's got some of my money." She handed me one of those safety pins with the number stamped across one end.

"You mean you came here with that . . . goon?"

"You don't approve? I guess I'll just have to check with you first from now on." She flipped her head like a spaniel, spraying me with water, and then headed off to the dressing room. "Meet you out front. Don't run off," she yelled back over her shoulder.

"You either," I called out.

The attendant didn't even blink when I checked out Dougie's stuff along with my own. I got dressed and went out front to wait. It was almost lunchtime, and my stomach was sending up messages, grinding away down there on imaginary munchies. The exhaust fan belched strange odors out of the snack bar, like french fries cooked in suntan lotion.

Heidi came around from the women's dressing room, shimmying her way into a pair of cutoffs. She handed me her bikini, still wet but mysteriously shrunken into two orange patches no bigger than a couple of Moist 'n' Dri Towelettes. She grabbed her hair in both hands and started twisting out the water.

"Give me his pants, Nelson." I had them tucked under my arm, still tightly rolled up. Heidi riffled through the pockets. She handed me a key chain with a tiny can of Coors beer, plastic, and three keys. She pulled a wallet out of the hip pocket and stuck it in her own back pocket without even giving it a look. Then she rolled the pants up again and stuffed them into a trash can planted at the building's corner under the exit sign. The can was green, with a message stenciled in white paint: "Give us a hand—please don't litter." Someone had painted in "job" after the word "hand."

"You drive?" Heidi asked.

"No, I hitched, walked part way," I answered.

"Good deal. Come on, we've got wheels now. You drive." She flipped me the keys, and I snapped them right out of midair, pure reflex. She took off for the parking lot, heading right straight for an electric-blue Firebird done up with racing slicks and whip antenna. This was beginning to look like grand-theft auto, and I wasn't quite ready to take the plunge.

"Hey, how well do you know this guy?" I asked, catching up. I still had the keys, and I wasn't opening up till I found out where things stood. "Look here, Heidi, the guy might be a creep, but you don't go ripping people off just for that."

Heidi's face hardened. "He knows my mother, or his mother knows my mother. I was doing them a favor, coming here with him. He thinks he's some big stud, but all's I know is he's here till Wednesday, then he has to go fix tanks in Germany or something. Look, if you want to be all faggotty about this, just give me the keys, and you can go back and hold his hand." Heidi was not exactly your girl next door, even if you live in a trailer park.

11

"Okay, look, get in and I'll take you home. But we go straight home and I bring this thing back." I unlocked the door and got in, reaching across to pop the other door open for Heidi. She slid in and started filching through the glove compartment right off.

"Want a cigarette?" she offered. I shook my head no.

"Good boy, huh?" she teased. She stroked an Ohio Blue Tip across the seat and lit up. Very dramatic. "About taking me home. . . . Problem is me and Mom don't get along. Had to move out till things . . . settle. Boyfriend problems—hers, not mine. Well actually, it's her boyfriend, my problem—can't stand his guts. He's unofficially moved in. I told Mom it was him or me, and the next morning they're squeaking away on the sofa bed. And she calls me the tramp. Really! I told you about him, I think. He owns the store."

"The guy with the dead cat?"

"Yeah . . . I think Mom's going for a raise."

"Really. And so where've you been?"

"Around. . . . First two nights at Elaine's—you know Elaine Mendoza, don't ya?" I didn't. "Then last night Dougie let me stay over, since his folks just spend winters here. So it's only three nights so far."

"You spent the night with Dougie? No wonder he was all over you! That rots, absolutely. Did he try to—"

"Don't worry about what he tried. . . . What are you so worried about? Who even asked you to butt in today? I can handle myself." She must have figured it was easier to go after me than to answer my question.

"Yeah, and so can everyone else. Drop it. Where you wanna head?"

"How about Mirabar Mall? All the comforts of home, except for beds. I need to pick up a few things anyway."

Mirabar Mall is one of those multimillion-dollar shopping extravaganzas modeled after the Pentagon. "Sure. I'll come back and meet you by Chip City after I ditch the car." Chip City had cookies big as hubcaps, and great benches, molded like tree trunks, for hanging around.

"Okay, just be careful. Dougie can really be a soreass." She snapped the cigarette butt out the window, and from the rearview mirror I watched it spin and slide along the white lines. We cut back toward Palmetto, and after a few miles' drive I cruised into Mirabar and dropped Heidi at the Sears entrance and headed back to Lake Marjorie.

I didn't bother looking for Dougie, I just stuck his car in the first empty space I could find and left the keys in the ignition. It wasn't five minutes before I caught a ride back to Mirabar with Mr. Garfein. He was a drafting teacher at the high school who used to break T squares over your head for mouthing off. A tough guy, a line coach with the varsity. He explained that in the summers he distributed cleaning supplies to motels, and spent most of his time on the road. I pretended to be interested in cleaning supplies until he started suggesting that maybe I'd be interested in working with him. He was hoping to become an Emerald, he told me. Which was like being an Eagle Scout in the company ranks. When he got to be an Emerald he could retire from teaching. He wanted my phone number, said we should discuss this some more. I told him our phone had been ripped out, but I wished him good luck at becoming an Emerald. By then we were at Mirabar. "Have a nice summer, what's left of it," Mr. Garfein yelled as I jogged across the sod into the parking lot.

It was pushing two when Heidi showed up. I'd had my fill of chocolate-chip cookies and was about ready to venture out on a search-and-destroy mission when I saw her staggering toward me, loaded down with bags and boxes from every store in the place. She dropped them in a heap on the bench beside me.

"Just hush till you see what I got," she said. I was ready to give her the third degree.

"Do you like sexy ears?" she asked, doing this slow-motion head turn like in the shampoo commercials. Her ears were red, with silver nubs stuck in each lobe. "Four ninety-five, pierced and everything. And they even throw these in." She fished a pair of huge silver hoops out of a white bag. "Hypoallergenic! Neat, huh?"

"Very foxy," I answered. "The buttons make you look a little Cuban."

"Look what else," she gushed.

We sat there on the plastic Chip City simulated tree stump and did the whole inventory. She had a cheeseball covered with nuts; pastel brassieres and a pair of underpants with a zipper painted on the front; three albums from Recordrama: "Iron Poor Blood," "Bottled Water" and "Clubfoot," which was also the name of the band; and a candle shaped like a horseshoe crab. There were three cartons of cigarettes, jeans and sweaters and a tape recorder, and a pair of knee-high boots, hand painted with crabs, from Taiwan.

"Zodiac boots, aren't they weird?" she said. "I'm a Cancer. Here's yours," and she thrust a small square bundle into my hands.

I unwrapped the thing, packed in a small white box with question marks over it. That was appropriate, because once I had it out, I still had no clue what it was. I mean, it was a little crystal ball stuck in the middle of sticks, all strung together in tight elastic cord.

"Figure it out." Heidi chuckled, all full of herself.

"What's to figure?" I said.

"It's a puzzle, dummy. You're supposed to get the ball out without breaking the sticks or pulling at the string."

"Oh, thanks," I answered, still confused. I started squeezing it, mashing it and mauling, like it was a real challenge and I had had the hots for a puzzle just like this ever since I hit puberty. What I was really trying to figure out was how Heidi managed to pay for all that stuff.

"Where's that wallet you slid into your pants, by the way?" I asked her point-blank.

"Gone, just like the money. Part was mine anyway. He owed me." She busily started shoving everything back into bags until it was all lumped together in three huge shopping bags.

"Come on, you'd better come with me," I said, giving it my best macho FBI inflection.

"The police???" she yelled, really angry. "You just try it!"

"No, home, with me. Give me those bags."

We waited outside in the shade with the ice-cream-eating grandmothers. Our bus was number nine, the Mirabar shuttle, Palmetto and the bypass. We got in and sat down, Heidi as brittle as ribbon candy beside me. What a case! She was a mystery, all right, and twice any puzzle you'd find in a gift shop. Problem was, I kinda liked her.

12

"Oh, yuk, the worms are coming out of his ears—*and his nose*! Grrrrrrrrrrrross." Heidi flinched in her seat, turning away and closing her eyes.

"Keep 'em closed. I'll tell you when it's over." I closed one eye myself and gave Heidi a little squeeze on her shoulder. It was our third really revolting movie in a week and a half. Heidi seemed to live for these things, and the more she couldn't watch, the better she liked the movie. We were going broke just trying to keep her horrified.

This one was *Bloodworm*. The ad said "You'll feel them crawling inside you" and showed this cuddly little worm coiled up in a globule of blood. What I actually felt was my stomach whirling around like a gyroscope. Some girl with strange psychic powers and an interest in biology kept implanting all these people with worm babies that sucked the

64

blood dry from inside out and then grew big and healthy as their hosts got anemic and wasted. Finally they'd come crawling out in search of more, more—they were insatiable, indestructible and very assertive. The girl was getting even with all these guys who wouldn't take her to the prom. But it all got out of control.

The first one, *Leprosarium*, had been heavy-duty rank, with all humanity being nibbled away, cell by cell, by some incurable strain of leprosy imported from outside the galaxy. But *Midway* was funny, the way all those rides got possessed and went on a rampage at the state fair, mangling and maiming. Imagine a Tilt-a-Whirl that growls.

"Thank God, is that it?" Heidi asked. She pulled herself up straight as the music swelled and the credits came sliding across the screen.

"Uh-huh. Wanna catch a burger?"

By the time we hit the parking lot we had accidentally fallen into step, like two GI's counting cadence. Heidi slipped her arm around my waist and was humming nonsense, "Cah-la-la tacha rumpty tumtoy tum diddle diddle dumling, how's your thumb." Another minute, I was afraid, and she'd have us skipping. But instead, she starts singing, inventing words, making up this sort of jump-rope song. That's when I found out I should never tell a girl my nickname.

"Half Nelson, Full Nelson, Nelson all the way,
Belson, Melson, Nelson, Schmelson, feed the boy some hay.
Feed him corn and carrots, put a pickle in his nose,
Put a candle in his pocket and some matches in his toes.
Put some dynamite beneath him and some cherry bombs, too,
And water them with gasoline—pow—Nelson, where are you?
Half Nelson, Full Nelson, Nelson all the way
Nelson here and Nelson there and Nelson's gone away."

She started over again, this time in a mocking whine right off the playground.

"All right, can it, that's enough," I warned in a desperate whisper. "You want everybody to think you're retarded?"

"Everybody who?" The parking lot was deserted, a few final cars stood at the exit waiting for the traffic to thin out.

Heidi started up again in her singsong voice. "Half Nelson, Full Nelson, wants to break your arm."

I joined the chorus, trying to drown her out. I took her wrist around my waist and spun out and under, locking her arm behind her, but it was only a soft one, gentle enough to get her turned around but hard enough to show I meant it. She curled around right into me, let her full weight drop flat against me until we were both ready to slam off balance right into the pavement.

I caught her under the arms and pulled her upright against me, throwing my right leg back as a brace. Her arms were around my neck, pulling me toward her with a slight pressure. She angled her head slightly to one side. By now it was totally unmistakable what was going on.

A straight-on kiss is a peck, strictly lip to lip, hit and run, suitable for grandmas and bye-byes at the bus station. I know all this now; I didn't know it then. What Heidi and I started with that night had a little more overlap, sort of dovetail, if you're into carpentry, or maybe tongue and groove. Either way, it was really incredible. Just like swimming—once you got it, you wonder how you never knew.

"There, got anything else to complain about?" Heidi asked as she pulled away.

"Can't think of a thing," I said, laughing. I held her, wanting to keep on but knowing I shouldn't wreck it, either. I just kept studying her face, thinking how much it was like one of those pictures where you had to spot the hidden objects, chipmunks and flowers and jelly rolls. That's when I decided she was pretty in spite of all the stuff I thought in period five. I think I even told her so right then.

"Now can we go home," she kidded, pulling me at arm's length toward the truck.

"We might as well. I'd like you to meet my folks." We jumped in the pickup and chugged off down the road for Gate o' Palms, keeping the joke alive—a simple wedding, honeymoon in the Bahamas, apartment overlooking the golf course, a fried-chicken franchise on the beach and three marvelous kids, twin boys and a girl with hair as black as Heidi's.

13

The trailer was black when we got home; not even the porch light was burning. That meant Dad hadn't made it back yet, must have missed his ride. Our note was still attached to the screen door, same masking tape and all. I saw Gram catch a peek out the kitchen, pulling the curtain back just far enough to let a slice of light slip out across the grass. Gram didn't like the arrangement, said it wasn't strictly proper to have a young girl living with two robust young men, as she called us. But it didn't bother Dad an iota. "You're welcome long as you can put up with us" is the way he said it the first time I came home ready with about fifty-seven different arguments as to why Heidi should move right in.

We fit together nicely, too. Partly it worked because Heidi was something new, not just a replacement part for a mother, wife or sister. She took up sleeping in Dad's

68

room on the box springs that were left after we decided that the mattress was too far gone to salvage. Me and Dad got the bunks, me still on top, Dad down below where Vanessa had been, a little cramped and sticking out around the edges like a ball of dough rising out of the bread pan.

The kitchen shift went on rotation after Heidi announced one night that she'd had her fill of my dad's no-fault over-easy fried eggs. She cooked Italian, mostly anything in sauce; I did cold cuts and anything out of a can; and Dad still hung tough with his fried eggs every third day. We got by.

Dad was killing himself for the General but feeling better about it all the time. He put new locks on the cages, rebuilt the monkey house and sodded around the flamingo pool. He'd come home exhausted every night and pass out after dinner, leaving us to drag him into bed. The money was a surprise—"right generous," he called it—however much that was. And the police were satisfied, looking for a way to settle up on what the chief started calling the Gator mishap. The General had pledged a sum to the wildlife refuge down the coast, and promised to hire a genuine naturalist curator first chance he got.

So after a few weeks it seemed that things were falling into place—getting back to normal—except now, normal didn't include Mom and Vanessa. Like two dead planets, me and Dad kept spinning along in our ragged orbits, reluctant to disturb the routine. Without a center, we were afraid we'd go skidding off course into oblivion. Mom had been that center. She had pulled at us, tugged us into place, scolding us, loving us—until she couldn't anymore.

And now it was my turn. She had said as much, telling me to take over and care for Dad, to be the new center filling in the emptiness she had left behind. Impossible.

We could keep on for a while, dancing our little family dance even after the music had stopped, but sooner or later it would become a shuffling two-step—to nowhere. And then what?

I kept troubling over how easy it is to just sit back and get used to any routine—like fried eggs every day, or horror flicks every weekend. The calluses harden up on your brain or your heart, and you adjust. Well, I wasn't gonna let that happen.

"Don't you guys ever change the sheets in here? Smells like an armpit." Heidi had chased me into the bedroom and fallen across the lower bunk into a tangle of sheets and pajamas.

"You're off limits anyways. This is men's quarters. Here," I said, ripping my bed apart. "We'll do these in the morning."

"Think you'd like to be a father, Nelson? Would you really know what to do with a kid?"

I wasn't convinced I'd heard that. I tried to catch her look, but her eyes were squeezed tight.

"A kid? Well, maybe after I'm married, it might be something to . . . What, are you—?"

"Suppose *we* had a baby, would you always, you know, care about us first?"

"Are we married?"

"Does it matter?"

"Well, to most people I suppose it does."

"Does it to you?"

"What are you getting at?"

"All right, look. Suppose I told my mother I was pregnant, suppose I told her you were the father."

"For real or pretend?"

"Either way."

"You mean lie about being pregnant, to your mother?" It was getting to be a slippery conversation, and I was looking for hard ground.

"Okay, something like that. Do you think it would make a difference?" She sat up and opened her eyes. "I mean, do you think she'd want me back enough then to throw that Mel guy out?"

"I don't even know your mother, Heidi," I answered. "Sounds drastic. Thought some girls get kicked out for stuff like that."

"That's just television."

"Whatever. I mean if I was the father, shouldn't I be the one to take care of you?"

"Suppose you ran off?"

That was about as far as I wanted to go. "Look, I wouldn't and you aren't, so let's just drop it. Besides, your mother'll probably give that guy the shaft before long. Anyway, how do you know you're not welcome back right now?"

"My mother's not exactly got the bloodhounds out after me. Think she gives a damn? She could have found me if she wanted me."

"C'mon, go easy, we want you here. Just think of this as a vacation. By the time school starts up again, probably everyone'll be back where they belong." I meant to include Mom and Vanessa in that, too, but school was only four weeks away and nothing was changing.

"Maybe if I were dead . . ." A strange light slid under her eyelids, like she was staring into a candle.

"Don't be morbid. Nothing's that bad."

"But what if she just *thought* something like that? Remember two years ago when those Boy Scouts disappeared at Tomalassassee Springs and the whole state went crazy? They had manhunts with dogs and skin divers, and the National Guard spent a week picking through the forest. . . ."

"Vaguely," I answered, trying to remember if those were the kids who turned up at a bus station in North Carolina, or just never got found at all.

"Look, we could go out someplace like that . . . take a picnic lunch and conveniently disappear. You call the police and report a missing person. Maybe a day later they get a ransom note."

"Yeah, saying 'Put ten bottles of fingernail polish and your disgusting boyfriend in a brown paper bag, drop it at the base of the fountain at the Wonder World Dog Track in the middle of the fourth race, and your daughter will be returned unharmed.' You'd never qualify. You're not the type, that's all."

"What's that supposed to mean? Nobody would give a damn what happened to me, is that it?"

"I would . . . but you gotta be rich or famous or, you know, an innocent little kid with hair ribbons. That's what gets everybody stoked up."

"Like that girl whose father owned the football team, yeah, she brought in a million bucks, imagine that. Turned out the guy worked for her father." She trailed off muttering under her breath.

My appetite was coming back after the movie. The refrigerator offered a toss-up between the leftover lima beans and a jar of maraschino cherries that had been pickling in their own juice since a New Year's party two years ago. Suddenly Heidi runs into the kitchen wrapped in a sheet like Miss Liberty.

"Vanessa, what about Vanessa?"

"What about Vanessa?" I ask.

"Kidnap Vanessa."

72

"She's my sister. Don't be ridiculous. You can't kidnap your own sister."

"Of course you can. It's perfect! It wouldn't be illegal, not with your own sister."

"But your mother wouldn't care about Vanessa. What good would it do you?"

"Suppose I was the kidnapper? Us together—I could write the notes and you could be my mystery companion. My mom, your mom and dad, they'd all be responsible. We're still minors, remember. The police would make them sit on us until we were eighteen."

"You're up a tree, if you ask me. What you need is a good shrink to get a little fine tuning. Now forget about it, it's crazy." I slammed the refrigerator door for punctuation. Bang. Drop it. End of discussion. It was absurd, asinine, half-baked, harebrained, dangerous and plain desperate.

Something desperate, I thought, and the word stuck in my ears, ringing like cymbals. Too farfetched. We'd need a car, some money, a hideout until Mom and Dad had time to worry a little, forget all the reasons they split and find better ones for getting back like before . . . and then, *April Fool*, nobody here but us kids, just maybe. . . .

14

Ten minutes later we're sitting at the kitchen table, looking at an Exxon road map of the state of Georgia. Somewhere in there, I figure, Mom and Vanessa are washing their hair or stacking their melamine dinnerware. I scan the directory of towns and cities. It's a big state full of mean-sounding names: Jesup, Valdosta, Nahunta, Waycross, even Jekyll Island. Nothing sounds familiar. We pull out a shoe box crammed with letters, old birthday cards, Christmas cards from way back. Mom kept everything. Still, there's nothing from Georgia. Nothing from Aunt Ruthie.

Could it all have been a smoke screen? No, there *was* an Aunt Ruthie. She did come for a week once—we went to the beach and cooked some ribs, and Mom sat talking to her all night, outside in the lawn chairs. She was a pinched and shrunken version of Mom, with harder eyes and a whiny, complaining voice. "Be nice to your Aunt

Ruthie," Mom coached us. "It hasn't been easy for her these last few years." That's as much as we ever knew, like that explained enough.

"Hurry, ditch the map, it's Dad." I scrambled to put the shoe box away while Heidi folded the map and shoved it back in the drawer. I tossed the shoe box back up into the cupboard, but it landed crooked, sliding back out and spilling into the sink. There was a loud roar, and a rumbling from outside, pulling into the drive. I raked the envelopes out of the sink, stacked them like a deck of cards, and gave them to Heidi to stow somewhere. I went to the door and snapped on the porch light. This wasn't Dad's ride. He usually came straight home with the groundskeeper in an old cherry-red VW. But that would have been hours ago. It was after ten now. He'd never been this late.

Then I saw it! Maybe five years old, still new as vans go, and fresh yellow metal-flake paint, with black trim. Across the side a huge lime-green alligator slithered with open jaws ready to strike. His tongue lashed out in a snarl, curling like he had a trace of Chinese dragon blood somewhere in his ancestry. Below the Gator jagged black letters spelled "GATOR MAN" and, below that, "of General Lee's Jungle Fever."

"Come on out here, Nelson," Dad called. He jumped down and smacked the door shut. "And get Heidi."

She didn't need the invitation. We were out there in a second, giving it the complete inspection. The other side was the same—incredible!—the colors had that spun-silk look that you can only get with an airbrush.

"We're in business, boy, we go on the road in a day. Pack something. You want to come along, Heidi? We're touring." Heidi stared, dumbfounded. "You coulda knocked me over with a toothbrush. The General sprung it all at once. He's got us some dates, and this here van is ours to use. Treat it nice, now," he adds as I start to open the rear doors for a look inside. "It's still the General's, sort of like a company car."

"Decent, man, really decent," Heidi was saying. She'd stuck her head in the front door, and we saw the bunk beds, the carpeted walls and the tape deck all at the same time.

"What a rig." Heidi was in shock.

"You mean you're a wrestler now, big time?" I kidded my Dad.

"Always was." He beams. "And you gonna be my road crew, Half Nelson and Miss Heidi and the Gator Man. Let's go in now. Gotta shave my head again. I'm a bad guy, gotta be ugly. We open at Pensacola come Thursday."

We followed him in, Heidi beside me, teasing again with her song: "Half Nelson, Full Nelson, Nelson all the way."

"We got to talk about that name. Just won't do. My Dad'll take some convincing, too," I said, remembering the promise I'd made to my mother. Heidi goosed me from behind, going up the stairs. We had a real mature relationship!

We turned up the radio and celebrated. Dad and Heidi danced around—shuffled, really, like a bear tied to a fox. Heidi burned some popcorn, we sipped beer (just a taste for a special occasion, Dad says, slapping a six-pack on the table—*chlink*) and Kool-aid. Dad's in great spirits, and we float up with him like we got hold of a hot-air balloon and can't let go. By midnight we're used up and ready for bed.

That night I lay on my bunk, ready to crash all night, with my Dad wheezing underneath me. My head was filled up to busting. Flat on my back, I ticked things off, like a pilot clearing for takeoff. When things got sorted out, I could turn over and sleep. Like, where am I going with Heidi? So we kissed, it felt good, does that mean we're

76

connected? Does that change us or do we forget it? Partly I could like her (*love her*—blah! "But why not?"), partly she scared me. With a girl like Heidi . . . ? (But what's Heidi like? And who cares and who counts besides me?) And my dad starting now, at last he's getting what he's wanted. What if Mom knew, and Vanessa, sleeping now somewhere in Georgia . . . but where? Would I slip through the window and carry her away, wrapped again in a blanket, asleep like the time they left? Yes, officer, I'm the girl's brother, Half Nelson, Full Nelson, Nelson all the way. . . . They're crawling inside me now . . . gators, the jungle's full of alligators . . . got the jungle fever and we're going to Pensacola Pensacola Pensacola Pensacola. . . . TILT.

But come the morning, I'm still awake, flat on my back and starting over for the ninety-ninth time.

UNBELIEVABLE MAT ACTION
A TOPFLITE
WRESTLING PROGRAM

The Pensacola Gulfside Armory Proudly Presents

ALL-STAR CHAMPIONSHIP WRESTLING CARD
Thurs., July 26, 8:00

● MAIN EVENT ●
for the Gulf States Heavyweight Championship

Bavarian Baron Von Braun		Val Augustine
Gulf States Champion	vs.	South-American Champion
264 lbs. (Germany)		252 lbs. (Colombia)

● SPECIAL EVENT ●
TAG TEAM CHAMPIONSHIP

The Astounding Samurai Brothers		Demolition Danny Demmons
combined weight, 486 lbs. (Japan)	vs.	237 lbs. (Rhode Island)
		Mark Antoro
		274 lbs. (Philadelphia)

● PRELIMINARY MATCHES ●

Ed "Warthog" Wardosky		Lance Loudermilk
283 lbs. (Chicago)	vs.	225 lbs. (Dallas)
The Terrible Rothgar		Danny Samuels
264 lbs. (Zagreb)	vs.	266 lbs. (Baltimore)
Seminole Sam Osceola		The Gator Man
246 lbs. (Miami)	vs.	272 lbs. (Sarasota)

15

"Hey, look, Gator Man, you're a star." I whooped, all of us coming into Pensacola with time to spare.

"Not hardly. Last man on the totem pole. That's what they call starting at the bottom." Dad was trying to sound bored with the whole thing, but I could see him glowing underneath. We had stopped for the red light at an intersection catty-corner from the Karsparkle Car Wash, and there was the poster, stuck up there on the telephone pole about six feet away.

It was a long light. "Chinese fire drill," Heidi yells, and she bolts out of the van, loops once around, and snags the poster—*chonk*—right back in the van just as the light turns green.

"Suitable for framing. Here, you take it," she says panting, jamming it into my lap.

We find the armory, a crumbly brick monster with little

castle turrets at each corner. It's in the low-rent district, for sure, crammed between a rusted-out warehouse and a plumbing supply house that was old probably before the invention of the flush toilet. Dad goes inside for about five minutes, then reappears with the General and some guy in a cowboy hat. The General had flown up the night before "to attend to details," as Dad said. The cowboy turned out to be the Topflite Wrestling promoter. He was a long piece of rope, all creases and lines, like he'd been made out of an old sheet of brown wrapping paper and sent through the mail.

Dad stuffed a wad of tens through the window. "Here's for a motel. Get something clean. . . . And you might as well eat. I'll see you after the match. Now, take care."

I took the money and wished him good luck. We'd be right there, I told him, so watch for us. Heidi pumped her fist out the window and yelled, "Go for it, Gator Man." Dad flashed her a wink, and the General came up behind him, waggling an index finger at us.

"Hold on, now," he was saying. "You all make sure you keep your receipts now, hear? These are expenses, gotta keep track of every penny, so don't go crazy. Now be good youngsters while your daddy and I go over the program with Mr. Larone here." Mr. Larone there tweaks the brim of his Stetson with a thumbnail. "Now mind what I say."

Yessir, uh-huh, yessir we agree, and we take off, me behind the wheel and Heidi waving backwards, saying "Blow it out your ear, coot." We cruise for a while, find a motel with color TV and vibramassage beds. We take a double room and stow our bags in the closet. For dinner we hit Maggio's Italian Villa—"Home of Better Pizza" the sign says. We split two mediums and decide the sign was right— the second pizza is better than the first. It's still two hours until the matches begin, so we head back through town and down along the shore drive. There's a naval air station nearby, and the place swarms with sailors. Heidi leans out the window to yell "Hey, Swabbie" every time she sees two or more standing together. I want to disappear, but Heidi keeps right up like she's head virgin in the Tournament of Roses parade. People hoot and whistle as we pass. It's the van, I realize, the incredible yellow metal-flake-plastered-with-alligators van.

"All riiiiight, Gator Man!" a sailor yells back.

"What it is, Gator Man, Sweet Machine," this little black kid hoots from the back of a BMX with bubble-gum tires.

We turn off into a development. Signs on every block warn SLOW CHILDREN AT PLAY, but the children stop playing as soon as we crawl by. They come chasing after us like we're the ice-cream truck. "Look at the scary crocodile." A little girl tugs at the hose while her mother waters the driveway. "Hey, mister," shouts some little twerp when we stop for a stop sign, "where's the circus? Give you five dollars for that hunk o' junk."

By seven we're lost. I idle at a 7-Eleven while Heidi goes inside to ask directions. "Just like we were going," she says, back inside the van. "Then right at some hospital until you come to the water, then left to the armory." It didn't exactly go like that, but in another half hour we'd found it anyway. We parked on the main street so no one would be tempted to use the van for target practice. It was that kind of neighborhood.

"Watch your van for a quarter, buddy," says this brown kid in swim trunks. He's got a bag of empties under one arm. I flip him a quarter, and he rattles it into his bag. "Thanks, pal," he says. He's barely seven, same as Vanessa, I think, and everybody's "pal" and "buddy." The kid shoots a hawker into the gutter. "Gross-out kid" Heidi calls him, but she giggles, like really it's cute. I grab Heidi and we head into the armory by the front entrance. A brass plate on the floor says "1907."

Pow!—the place smacks you right in the nose. You walk past the bathrooms stinking of wine and peecakes. The dust is so thick it slides up your nose, burning like pepper, with just enough oil to make it smell like an abandoned garage. Heidi sneezes, five short bursts.

We walk up to the ring, a huge box of candy built of new lumber, pine two-by-fours, the only fresh smell in the building. Above the ring four banks of lights, like huge inverted ice-cube trays, hang down on chains. Between them, a thick black cord with a microphone at the end dangles, twisting slowly in some invisible draft. Suddenly the lights flicker on, casting a white glare. I check the time—seven-twenty.

We sit in some chairs three rows back from ringside. Heidi stretches her feet over the chair in front of her and lights a cigarette. "So where *is* everybody, anyhow?" She tilts her head back and exhales, letting the smoke float up to mix with the dust.

"They'll show up. It's still early. Maybe they only come for the main events." But the place is nearly empty.. Some kids share homemade popcorn on the top row of the bleachers. A woman with sagging arms front row center licks green stamps, sticking them in a book. Others start to show. Five guys in their twenties come down the aisle, mostly stoned. They go up to the ring and start pulling on the ropes. One jumps in the ring. "C'mon, take all you mothers," he's yelling. The others grab him out of the ring and they all swagger into chairs opposite us and settle down, passing around a joint.

By eight the crowd is maybe 150, but wretched types, Salvation Army material. The armory resembles one of those disaster relief centers, where people straggle around waiting for the Red Cross to hand out blankets and soup. It's after eight-fifteen when this little man in a red tuxedo struggles into the ring. His black hair is slicked over a bald scalp, and his cheeks are red circles—Heidi says it's rouge. He pulls the microphone down and starts reading off a card folded into his hand. Nothing. He spits into the microphone—*screeeeeeeeee*—and the armory echoes with feedback. Then again he reads, with an accent right off the banana boats:

"Ladies and gentulllllman, The Pensacola Armree and Topflite Wrestling welcome chou to a evening of strordinary wrestling action. Tonight's main event fitchures the Barbarian Baron bersus the Bal Augustine. But first, we begin for chou with a cupple newcomers in our first ebent. From Miami, out of the Eberglades reserbation, Seminole Sam Osceola will meet the Gator Mon, who wrestles out of Sarasota."

Automatic boos welcome the referee, a stumpy man with eyebrows like black caterpillars. "You stink, DeNucci," someone yells, but he's too busy pulling up his pants and checking his fly to notice.

Then Sam and the Gator Man bound into the ring like they're shot from catapults. Sam jigs up and down in moccasined feet, doing a little war dance. His hair is thick and black as Heidi's and done in braids. He has copper arm bands jammed over his biceps, and a little Indian loincloth with bib front and back that flaps with every jig. So does the little roll of butterfat around his waist, jiggling wildly despite the blanket draped over his shoulders for camouflage. He tilts his head back, all noble and hawklike. He isn't none of that stuff is the only problem—strictly Hollywood Injun routine, far as I can figure.

The Gator Man comes stormin'. General Lee follows him into the ring stroking his bone-white head, like he's soothing a wild beast. Then the General proceeds to get into this argument with referee DeNucci. He points to a chair at ringside, the General points to the Gator Man, the Gator Man points to Sam, who's still jiggling up and down, ignoring the whole thing. Finally the General sits down ringside, leaning on his knob-top walking stick, while the Gator prowls the ring, stalking Sam in a crouch. "Corners, gentlemen," DeNucci shouts. Sam obeys, skipping to his corner. The Gator skulks after him. "Corners," DeNucci shouts again at the Gator, stamping his foot on the mat and pointing. The Gator takes a swipe at DeNucci, gets only air, then retreats to his corner.

"Is your old man cracked? Listen to him, he's growling," Heidi says, punching me in the ribs first to get my attention.

"That's all part of it. Just watch!" I tilt forward in my seat to ecape Heidi's questions.

"Part of what?" I heard her ask under her breath. The two men circle the ring, winding toward each other in a tightening spiral. The Gator Man's left arm extends like a rifle point-blank in Sam's face, the fingers spread and cocked into a talon. The other hand fidgets with the shoulder strap, tugging and adjusting at the leopardskin strap that keeps sliding down around his elbow. Then both wrestlers rear and lock ear to ear with their heads cradled on the other's shoulder.

"C'mon, wrestle you bums!" Someone shrieks from behind us.

"Look, they're dancin' like gayboys," the green-stamp lady snarls from across the ring.

84

Then *pow*, the Gator's down on one knee, holding Sam at arm's length in a lock around the wrist. He stands and winds it up. "Three . . . four . . . five . . . six." The crowd counts along as he rotates the arm, twisting up and over a full turn each count until Sam's face contorts into a silent scream. The Gator Man rams his foot up under Sam's arm-pit, still pulling on the arm like it'll pop out easy as the drumstick on a boiled chicken. Sam's face deepens three shades redder to excruciating. He drops to the mat, pulling the Gator Man off balance onto his back. Sam pounces—forearm smash—to the face, to the chest, knee drop to the throat, then spreading his legs in a wishbone.

The Gator Man goes limp. He stares wildly around the ring, looking into the crowd for mercy, forgiveness. Sam drags him to the corner, handling him like he's a lifeless doll. Sam smashes the Gator Man's head against the turn-buckles again and again. The ring shakes, the ropes whirl wild as clotheslines in a gale. The Gator Man droops to the floor, dazed, blinking into the lights. Sam goes into his dance, arms above his head, as the crowd whoops like a band of warrior braves.

"Get up, Gator," Heidi screams. "Get after him, now, come on."

I watch the Gator Man sitting slumped in the corner, his feet twitching in his cracked black boots. Sweat runs from his sleek pale scalp and drips from his chin onto the leopardskin suit. Already it is dark, drenching in the thick air. His eyes are unfamiliar, sad and bruised. They seem to stare inward. "John Anthony Gato," I whisper to myself, "John Anthony Gato," as though I am sitting at a séance raising dead spirits from beyond. The man in the ring doesn't move.

"Wrestle, get up and wrestle," Heidi calls along with the crowd.

The Gator Man pulls himself up on the ropes. He hurls himself at the prancing Seminole and catches him on the chin with a flying dropkick. He follows with an attack of knee drops to the gut and the neck, slamming onto the mat with thundering force. The Gator Man swarms over Sam, lashing him with elbows, knees, then pulls him upright to catch him with a burst of head butts, using his shaven head like a wrecking ball. "Foul," someone cries. Others hoot "Dirty wrassler" but the Gator Man keeps it up, ignoring the catcalls. Referee DeNucci flutters around them, confused.

Suddenly the Gator Man turns on the crowd. He leaves Sam crumpled in center ring and walks to the ropes with his fist clenched in a dare. The green-stamp lady stands up and takes a looping swing at midair with her shopping bag. The Gator Man lunges like he's going to jump the ropes after her. The crowd shrieks, hysterical with delight.

A small man at ringside stands to toss something, a stick, into the ring. It's the General! The Gator Man picks the walking stick off the canvas and, whirling it above his head, comes down with a conk on the back of Sam's head. Sam, who had just managed to struggle to one knee, collapses like a tent. The Gator Man falls on top, with the stick slipped under Sam's chin, across his Adam's apple. With the stick now cradled in his elbows and his hands clasped behind Sam's neck, the Gator Man pulls Sam upright and forces the stick deeply into the Indian's neck. Sam's head starts lolling back and forth, his tongue hangs wildly out the side and his arms drag limp, useless, at his sides.

"Throw him out, disqualify the bum," a voice screams, setting off a chorus of protest. "Stop it, stop the match" the chant begins. I turn to see Heidi rocking in her seat beside me, chanting right along.

Obediently, it seems, DeNucci steps in at last, delicately prying the two men apart. The Gator Man finally gives in and steps back to celebrate his victory, both arms raised high overhead. But instead, DeNucci holds Sam's arm straight up in the air—"the winner!" Sam is rejuvenated enough to go into his little Seminole victory dance. The Gator Man leaps straight up and then rages around the ring at the injustice, threatening DeNucci himself with the notorious walking stick. The General scrambles into the ring to join the protest, railing back at the heckling crowd. But it's over, DeNucci shoos the General out of the ring, and the Gator Man follows, now suddenly calm as he jogs behind the General up the aisle to the dressing room. He dodges to avoid the slaps and jabs of the taunting fanatics.

"Sorry, Nelson. Looks like he freaked again. Maybe he's just not cut out for this stuff, the pressure and all." Heidi kneads my leg to make me feel better. It barely helps.

"No, not this time. He was okay. Matter of fact, pretty good for a debut. Didn't you hear the screaming? They wanted to string him up by his gonads. You did, too, about three minutes ago, remember?"

"I don't get what you mean. He lost, he was disqualified. He went absolutely bananas. How can you . . . ?"

"SSSSShhhhh . . . listen." I point to the ring. The little man in the red tuxedo is pulling down the mike.

"The winner of the first mash at six twenty-seven into the round, by the disqualification by the referee . . . Seminole Sam Osceola."

The crowd murmurs, now almost indifferent. The armory is filling; the crowd seems to get more civilized as it grows. The first match has already been forgotten. Two fresh wrestlers enter the ring wearing these really elaborate satin robes, embroidered and studded with sequins—obviously they've been on tour for a while.

"Never mind what I mean right now. You'll catch on after we've been to Mobile, Shreveport and Jacksonville," I say, naming off the other stops on our tour. We change seats just for something to do, and last for a few more matches before a security guard comes up and whispers that Dad is waiting for us in the van. We talk very little that night on the way back to the motel. Heidi seems nervous around him, while I can't get past this formal feeling, like I couldn't be the son of that strange man I'd seen in the ring. Dad is too tired to notice.

Things loosened up a good bit by the time we hit Jacksonville. The matches had all gone pretty much the same way. Everybody was really hating the Gator Man, and the General was very pleased. Finally, midway through his match on that last night in Jacksonville, the same night we drove straight on back to Palmetto, Heidi turns to me and says, almost like it's an apology, "It's really all just like a comic book, isn't it?"

"Something like that," I agree. "Only here they use real people."

16

Dearest Nelson,

Ever since I left I been wondering about how you might be doing. I promised I'd let you know how we made out, and Vanessa must worry me half to death with her "Nelson this and Nelson that" until I could scream. She says she has trouble going to sleep now that her big brother isn't sleeping up above in the old bunk bed.

You'd probably like it here at Ruthie's. There's lots of nice boys your age right around here. Ruthie has a hair studio built right onto her house, and she's just filled up with appointments all day long. Some of the most fashionable ladies in Crosswell just think she's so wonderful. She has another girl working for her, but she lets me help out some, too, shampooing and all that simple stuff. I'm even taking beauty courses at night so that pretty soon I can have a license.

You must realize that your father and I have gone as far together as we could go. In a few more weeks he will be getting a letter from a lawyer I have talked to about getting a divorce. This will be very hard on your father, and you must stand by him just as strongly as I tried to for almost seventeen years. It is just a tragic thing, but necessary if we are to go on with our lives. Always remember that you are my son forever. You and Vanessa are both such wonderful strong people that I know you will always do well. Try to understand a little about this now, and maybe years later you will see why it had to happen.

I want you to promise that you will stay a good person. Do your best in school and keep yourself clean. Your whole life is ahead of you. I know how you hate gushy things, but you must know that I'll always love you. And Vanessa will always love you, too. When these things settle over, there will be time for us to get together. Be extra strong and help your father through this for me.

All my love,
Mom

P.S. Vanessa's school medical records are in the old shoe box in a school envelope. Please send them. I need to register her for school in September.

Sometimes you get so scared your mind can't deal with it—that's when your body takes over, giving all that misery an outlet. I could feel the sickness filling me up inside, wringing me around down deep from my heart to my stomach. "Lawyers, medical records, years later, always love you" . . . damn, that sounded permanent, terminal, good-bye forever and thank you very much. Well, pardon me, Mother dear, but Nelson Gato flunked out of obedience school a long time ago, exactly because he could never get the part right where you have to roll over and play dead.

And you don't just take a guy's sister away like she's a mahogany end table or something, because not even a mother has exclusive rights to somone's sister. I'm not talking legal rights, either. I'm talking the kind of rights where you teach a kid how to whistle, or jump rope backwards, or catch minnows with a sieve. Those are a brother's rights, and they've got to count for something or there's no use sharing the same blood and genes and bathroom.

So get all the lawyers you want, I decided, get battalions of them, hordes and swarms of lawyers, and stand them up linked arm in arm, 'cause red rover, red rover, old Nelson's comin' over and the three-piece suits are gonna fly. . . .

Suddenly, from outside, voices slid into my rage. I folded the letter back up and jammed it in with the rest of the mail that had come while we were away. The General was talking, but it was all coming in a blur.

". . . exposure . . . reach a national audience . . . The Gator Man will become a household name. . . . It's a once-in-a-lifetime opportunity, and if it goes well they can extend our contract for even more television. How about it, boy, you ready to see your daddy wrassle on TV?"

"Uh, TV, no kidding, hey, that's great," I mumbled, with all the enthusiasm of a gravedigger.

"Say what, boy?"

"Great, I said it's really great."

"Great, hell, it's fantastic." Dad practically skipped across the floor. "Show a little enthusiasm, Nelson."

"I said it's wonderful, whadda ya want, cartwheels for chrissake?"

The General got up and spit in the sink. "Damn kids," he muttered under his breath. I excused myself and went to the bathroom, still holding the bundle of mail. I locked the door, stuck the letter at the bottom of the clothes hamper, then sat down and got very sick—or maybe I just thought I got very sick. Sometimes it all comes down to the same thing.

"Lie still," Heidi was saying, "the doctor said you can go home in the morning." Her face was bending down into mine.

"What doctor?"

"No doctor, dummy, that was a joke."

I was stretched out on the box springs in Heidi's room. I could hear my heart beating in back of my ears.

"Where's everybody?" I asked.

"Gone to Sarasota. Your dad's gonna get one of those satin robes, custom-made. The General knows a tailor from Vietnam."

"The General knows everybody. Sit down here." I patted the bed beside me. "We got some problems to discuss."

"You gonna pass out again? We figured you had the Legionnaire's flu, or something. You better now?"

"Yeah, better, and a whole lot worse. That's what I want to talk about." I sent her into the bathroom to retrieve the letter. She read the whole thing straight through without blinking.

"Sounds like she means it."

"I think she does. And not a word about it."

"Sure . . . but sooner or later . . ."

"The lawyer, yeah, I know. They take time, that's why we gotta mobilize now. It's only two weeks till school."

"That reeks."

"So do you want to be in on it? You can scout around, you know, without getting spotted. If Mom saw me, that would blow the whole ball game. You up to it?"

"Believe it. Don't forget, I'm the founding member of the abandoned-baby club. My old lady thought of it first. She's got at least a month's head start on your mother."

"Well, at least my mother . . ." I was gonna say "didn't leave me for a nail-polish tycoon," but that would have hurt, so I shut up.

"Your mother what?" she asked.

"My mother left a forwarding address," I offered, weakly.

"Well, your mother, my mother, same difference. If we make big enough waves we can get them both wet, flush 'em right out of hiding. So, sure, we partners or what?"

"Sure, partners," I said, extending my hand. She ignored it, surprising me with a hug instead.

"Don't worry, Nelson. We'll be great together," she added, her voice suddenly shading into a whisper. Then just as suddenly she let go and fell backwards onto the bed. An invitation? I spun and started pacing the room, all business.

"Good. It'll take a little planning, of course. We'll need money, some wheels, uh, a place to hide out until things develop. Maybe we should sit down and kinda draw up a list or a—"

"Disguises, we should have disguises." Heidi bucks up off the bed and starts shuffling through Mom's abandoned dresses in the closet.

"She leave these for a reason?" she asks.

"Naw. Dad says it shows she means to come back. But all it really shows is that she took off out of here like a blue streak."

"How about this one, a cute burgundy?" Heidi says mostly to herself. She hooks the hanger over the top of the closet door. I'm getting ready to explain how basically stupid it is for her to use one of my mother's own dresses for a disguise when Heidi backs out from behind the door slipping off her shorts and then yanking off her top. I'm sitting there on the bed like this is absolutely the most natural everyday occurrence, like toast for breakfast. But look, I mean Heidi was right there maybe eight feet away in nothing but those underpants and she was, after all, semibeautiful.

Of course, this was a first for me, and I know all along that physical attraction, the bod and all that, is only a small part of liking someone. Like there's inner beauty and intelligence and all that stuff, as Ann Landers or Kenny Rogers or somebody once said. But in Heidi's case this was sort of the deciding vote along with all the other weird reasons I was thinking I liked her. And from then on, something started ticking away inside, some primitive tribal impulse started bubbling away like before long it would take over. But for Heidi it was just like dress-up time in the attic. Maybe it was the first dress she had ever worn.

"Like it? It's a little big."

"It's gorgeous," I answered, referring more to Heidi than to the dress. My knees and elbows felt wrung out. Everything else went stiff. I'm glad I didn't have to get up and walk right then.

17

The next day we took the van into Sarasota. Dad was going to pick up his robe and wanted our opinion. We stopped at the Astoria Diner. The cook was an old navy buddy, and Dad insisted we try his world-famous smoked mullet and garbanzo bean soup. The food was okay, but the menu should have been printed on flypaper. Heidi lifted two ashtrays and a saltshaker shaped like a cactus. I made her put the saltshaker back. She was wearing her hypoallergenic hoop earrings and a bandanna wrapped around her head, gypsy-style. When she walked down Cypress Boulevard side by side with the massive Gator Man, his head twinkling in the afternoon sun, you had to check the intersections to see where the caravan was parked.

A man pulled a camera out of his "Elkhart VFW" Windbreaker and asked them for a pose. "Over there by the palm tree, if you don't mind"—he gestured them toward the edge of the sidewalk—"just so they know it's really Florida." He thanked them and asked if they were with the circus. "We are Tasha and Taru, de Human umbrellas," Heidi answered. The man left satisfied and went off in search of pelicans.

About a block before we came to the tailor's, Dad detours us right into this crumbling shop doorway. The window is painted black, but once inside, we see that it's a kind of jewelry store. A banner hanging behind the counter says "Aztec Artisans," and sure enough out walks this sleek dude wrapped in a leather headband, twice the Indian Seminole Sam could ever hope to be. "They ready?" my dad asks, and the Indian nods, reaching under the counter and producing three white boxes, each about the size of a can of Spam. Dad takes the boxes and hands one to me and one to Heidi.

"Here's for you two," he says. "Open them. They're to keep our luck running to the good. And thanks for sticking by me, for maybe being my good luck, you know."

Heidi tears into hers and pulls out a shiny lump all wrapped around in cotton. It's pure silver, an alligator hardly bigger than a baby lizard, with eyes studded out of two pieces of turquoise.

"Oh, wow, he's adorable, he really is," Heidi says. She loops her arm around the Gator Man's neck and tries to plant a kiss on his cheek but can only reach his chin.

I open my box—it's the same silver gator, except with these really jet-black eyes, downright sinister.

"Obsidian," the Indian says.

"Obsidian—that's lava rock," Dad explains. "Now you bring that with you this weekend when we go up to Macon. It'll be our television charm, better than any mangy old rabbit's foot you could dig up anywheres. Now promise."

96

"Macon . . . you mean the Macon in Georgia?" That would be perfect, I was thinking, right into the eye of the hurricane. I could hardly wait to get back home and dig out the map.

"How many Macons you know of, Nelson?" Dad chuckles. "Of course the one in Georgia. We tapin' this Saturday, 'live on tape,' like they say. Which means I'll be showin' up all over the country sooner or later. S'posed to do one of those ringside interviews, too. The General insisted and Mr. Larone said okay. So we gotta get something crazy ferocious like how all those name wrestlers do it. General says it's all in the presentation. Your Valentines, your Ivan Koloffs, Mascaras, they all got a way with words like a carnival barker. You two think about it, maybe you can whip me up a little speech. Nasty and memorable."

"No problem," I agree, watching him twirling the third box in his hand. "That one for you?" I ask him, staring at his hand.

"No sir, this here one's for Vanessa, sort of a 'welcome home' gift. 'Course, it'll have to wait until Ness and your mother come back, but I figure that once Old John Gato has got hisself together and all, they'll give up on their little walkout and come right back where they belong. Don't you have faith that they will, Nelson?"

"Yes, sir, I have faith," I answer, amazed that such a word ever made it into his vocabulary. But then, maybe that's what helped pull him along for all the years when there was nothing left.

I give Heidi a look until I see her face wrinkle into a wicked smile—my co-conspirator. She turns away before Dad can catch on to the undertow at work, pulling us all into the deep water back up in Georgia, ready to sink or swim.

"Mighty fine work, Frank. Thanks a whole bunch," Dad says, handing the Indian a check. We leave the store, Dad bouncing along on the balls of his feet and whistling like he's auditioning for the Seven Dwarfs. "Best feeling around, Nelse," he says between choruses of tweets and chirps. "Just walking right in and paying for something, having it all yours free and clear, yessirbygod."

Duc Tho, pronounced Duck Toe, greeted us with a "happy afternoon" from behind a window full of broken jalousies. It was a happy afternoon, I thought then, probably the best feelings all around since long before Mom and Vanessa had gone. Heidi was half believing she was a gypsy and Dad was flat out giddy with that feeling of things going right for a change. His biorhythms were peaking out.

We got the "Hong Kong shore leave" story about fried monkey for breakfast and the entire gamut of Three Stooges snarls and honks. He even gave Heidi his famous tribute to the "legendary Elvis," flexing his upper lip until it looked like a twisted snail migrating to his right ear.

"Wuh-hell, you-hoo tuh-reat me luh-hike uh fuhoooollll
Tuh-reat me mean and cuh-roooool
Buh-huh-huh-huh-hut luh-huv me. . . ."

So it wasn't any wonder that old Duc Tho just stood there slack-jawed when he saw us skip up his steps and waltz around in his living room, the three of us arm in arm, like we'd just been evicted from the yellow brick road. It was strong stuff, I gotta admit it now, but sometimes when the mood is right you can really weird people out. It's the best therapy around. Unless you get that way permanent. I figure when you can't switch it off is when they start drafting the commitment papers. Then you lock into being the Cowardly Lion or the legendary Elvis or Tasha the Gypsy, and there's no way out.

"These here are my fashion consultants, Mr. Tho," Dad says, waving an arm in our direction. "You got her all stitched up?"

"Yes. I get for you. Try on? Hope you find it to enjoy." Tho walks sideways through a curtained doorway. For a tailor he sure is no fancy dresser—his pants billow and flap, while his shirt blouses out like an inflated pillowcase.

"You try it on now, children can see," he says when he returns with the robe folded across his forearm. He shakes it out and it fills with air like a spinnaker catching a stiff breeze. It seems to float onto Dad's arms, up onto his shoulders, almost liquid, then settles in gentle folds until he looks like a great reptile Pope. The robe is green like new grass, and across the back a darker green alligator, modeled after the one on the van, is sewn on with delicate overlapping stitches. Embroidered in black thread, the words "Gator Man" arc just above the gator.

Dad shoots a look over his right shoulder as he backs up to a mirror to catch the whole effect.

"naM rotaG" he reads off the mirror. He pulls the belt tight around his middle and holds the tip ends straight out from his waist. After holding that pose he starts swishing around, sashaying his hips. Split my gut, I swear, and Heidi's singing, "Oh, there he is, walking on air he is, Mis-ter Ga-tor Man," while this nearly three-hundred-pound man, my own father, tippy-toes around, posing front and back like he's on the ramp in Atlantic City. He sweeps by Heidi and lifts her right off the floor, and they go spinning off around the room ready to levitate right into midair.

"Mr. Gator finds the gown satisfactory, you sink?" Duc

Tho whispers to me as he shrinks away from the whirling couple.

"Yes, sir, very satisfactory," I tell him. "It's beautiful."

"Beauty-full, tiss is what I am hoping for, good." Tho applauds himself and hops off the floor like a cheerleader. Dad and Heidi have broken into a modified polka, laughing, with their heads tilted back and their knees chopping up and down with each step. I cut in on Dad just to save Heidi from being smashed into the carpet. We dance out onto the porch. "Let's go," I shout, and Dad follows us out the door, still wrapped in the satin robe.

Okay, so imagine a bald man of approximately Incredible Hulk proportions jogging in a green satin robe down a main thoroughfare of a semifamous Florida town followed by two deranged and panting teenage wrestling groupies. Soon we've picked up kids, dogs, joggers on Medicare and a squadron of skateboarders swooshing in formation. Magnetism, presence, pin a label on it for the General. Anyway, before long we've formed a tight little mongrel band, flapping down the sidewalk and across the pavement.

Then we hear the rattle of a siren wailing in its lower registers. A big Electraglide Harley slows alongside us and cuts the Gator off at an intersection. The cop gets off and smiles like a cowboy, creases jumping to attention all over his face. The crowd bunches up, joggers still running in place. The cop removes his helmet and tucks it under his arm, astronaut-style.

"You got a parade permit for this here situation, fellow?" the cop asks.

"This ain't no situation, officer. We're just, you know, stepping along, stretching our legs and our lungs. These two here are with me," he says, pointing to me and Heidi. "The rest is just tagalongs. Sure ain't no parade."

"Well, maybe not, but I'm afraid there is a municipal ordinance that requires a permit for gatherings of a substantial nature along the city's major arteries. Now, friend," the cop puts a hand on my dad's shoulder, real confidential, like he's having a fine time just getting a chance to display his official training in front of so many good citizens—"you gotta understand that we're tryin' to do a job. What you got here is some kind of potential unlawful assembly."

"Poop," says my dad.

"That's real cute. Now how about lettin' me see some ID." The cop spreads his legs like it's time to get down to business. Heidi pushes by me and starts staring at the cop's badge, probably so she can call the commissioner to file a complaint about brutality. The crowd begins to disappear as Dad hands over his wallet. I begin transmitting brain waves to my dad—composure, composure, let's not blow it this time. I stare right into the back of Dad's head.

"John Anthony Gato" the cop recites from the wallet. He looks up again. "Well, Mr. John Anthony Gato, you some kind of prizefighter or something? You better train somewheres else in that getup; people gonna think you makin' a movie. Turn around there now, let's take a look."

My dad spins around, fanning the robe out like he's Count Dracula.

"Gator Man, now ain't that somethin'," the cop purrs. "Now why don't you just take that pretty thing off and proceed on back to your swamp, real orderly, and we'll just chalk this one up to good times. And no more showboatin'. I think you get my point, now, don't you?"

"I suppose so. It's your city. I still don't see the harm in a few folks lettin' loose a little, but, hey, you're the officer in charge and you're just trying to do the best you can. No harm in that, sir." Dad sounds like a recorded message

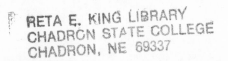

finishes it off with a salute. Apparently satisfied, the cop hands back the wallet and straddles his bike, flipping a salute back over his shoulder as he zooms off.

"I'da wrapped him around his motorcycle, the little twerp," Heidi rages.

"No use in griping, Heidi," Dad says, folding his robe. "They got you if they want you. Just agree 'em to death and throw in a few 'sirs.' Softens 'em right up." He was getting kind of expert at these matters, I decided then. Used to be he'd bristle up like an old alley cat and scratch right back. But he wasn't weakening, not really—just catching on to how to survive. Gators were good at surviving, I figured. A few years back the gators were an endangered species, overhunted, trapped for pocketbooks and shoes and trophy cases. But they were coming back now, protected and regulated, but still wild things.

But Heidi kept right on steaming anyhow, like she had sort of inherited all the old leftover anger that would normally have kept the old Gator growling for days. Dad was all mellowed out again, like you'd never have known it all happened. We got back to the van and took off for Rudy's Servicenter, where we had an appointment for a tune-up, points and plugs, and maybe adjust the valves. "Get her shipshape, Rudy. We're going on the road again, playing a TV date in Macon," Dad had to slip it all in. Rudy didn't know from Adam what that meant, but he nodded anyhow. We could of been a late-summer tour on the Donkeyball circuit for all he cared.

"Give me two hours and she's yours," Rudy promised. I checked the clock and gave Heidi a nudge. We'd be getting back late, and we still had a lot of strategy to work out before hitting Georgia.

We found a tavern that catered to the racetrack crowd

and dug into a booth to do a little more heavy-duty pigging out. We polished off some meatball subs washed down by some apple beer. Heidi got hooked on an air hockey game, and we used up a fistful of quarters before switching over to Zaxxon. I racked up over 56,327 points by concentrating on smashing the 500-point mother ship starcruisers and was declared the undisputed champion of the intergalactic space wars. After an hour and a half of that, we declared the tavern a party zone, and Dad popped for two pitchers of beer.

Sogginess was taking over my brain when Dad starts proposing toasts to the health of the younger generation. "To Heidi and Half Nelson Gato, two fine young Americans, and a couple of great kids in the bargain," he says, lifting his glass into the air above us.

But I refuse to lift my glass. "Dad, could we drop the Half Nelson routine?" I ask, remembering Mom's request about the old nickname.

"Half Nelson routine?" he repeats, stunned. "But hey," he brightens—"come on, old man, don't go getting sophisticated on me. I love ya, kid, and you don't leave me many ways to show it."

"Oh, never mind, it's nothing." I retreat, feeling dumb.

"To the Gator Man," Heidi blurts out, coming to my rescue, "the scourge of the universe and the baddest man on the mat." She chinks her glass against mine and dumps half the beer in my lap.

"And to tomorrow," I add in my turn.

"Yes, that's good, to tomorrow, and to us," Dad bellows, filling up the tavern with his voice.

18

So here it is, for the record, the authentic "don't mess with the Gator Man" blood oath and all-out Godzilla boast. As composed by yours truly, Nelson Gato, Esquire, on the way to Georgia, with special thanks to the delightful Miss Heidi Tedesco. And as memorized and performed by the terror himself, John Anthony Gato, aka the Gator Man.

I'm a bad, nasty son of an alligator,
A swamp-stomping, monster-chomping mutilator,
An eye-gouging full-grown brain agitator,
A cold-blooded criminal law violator,
A bone-crushing, hair-pulling face annihilator.
I'm the outlaw plastic surgeon, the bone obliterator.
And you're all in wicked trouble with the Gator, now or later!

Well, it might not be "The Night Before Christmas," but with the Gator Man woofing it out, totally deranged, not fifteen feet away from the glare of the TV lights, it all had a kind of sincere ring to it. Good old Vince Deloria, your personable ringside announcer, stood there with the mike stretched out at arm's length. He pulled back a little to avoid getting bitten, and the Gator Man leaned his face into the mike. He began making up a tirade against his opponent, Samson Florentine. Never mind that he's never heard of him before—his eyes roll and bulge like two hard-boiled eggs, spit popping off the mike the way bacon grease explodes in the pan:

"The Florentine is a woman, a weak-kneed, chicken-hearted, drooling greaseball who isn't man enough to polish my boots with his miserable tongue. He is trash, he is scum, he is a boil on the armpit of the universe, the ugliest man to ever climb into the ring with the divinely gorgeous Gator Man. And after today he will be even uglier. I will rearrange his face to look like a bowl of last year's tuna salad. I will tie his legs into granny knots and braid his plug-ugly fingers like rope. I will use his eyes for marbles and bite off his nose and spit it back in his face. I will grab that whiny moronic son of a pencil-necked geek by his ears and snap his little pinhead right off his shoulders just like this. . . ."

And with that the Gator Man grabbed Vince by the ears and began twisting back and forth until General Lee jumped into the action long enough to loop a towel around the Gator Man's neck from behind. He pulled him, raving like a banshee, back toward the ring.

Vince coughed into the mike, checking to make sure his voice still worked. He adjusted the knot on his tie and slid the hand up to his Adam's apple, molding it into place like a lump of flattened putty. He sputtered something under his breath in soprano. Finally, he looked the camera straight on and wheezed his way through a wrap-up: "As you can

105

see, fans, the Gator Man is just about ready for his match with Samson Florentine. And frankly, I pity the Florentine if he has to get into the ring with the Gator in such an ugly frame of mind. We'll be watching it all from right here at ringside. But before we get to that exciting wrestling action, let's take this commercial time-out."

As the lights dimmed and the camera retreated back up the aisle, I took off to look for Heidi. Something was keeping her. Not ten minutes after we hit the auditorium in Macon, she'd slipped out the dressing room door after whispering something about "arrangements." We were planning to leave for Crosswell in the middle of the Gator's match to avoid any complicated explanations. Our whole plan depended on staying one step ahead of the bloodhounds—problem was that was as much plan as there was. I'd made copies of the keys to the Gator Van, but it would've been disastrous to swipe that. It was still in the General's name, and besides, once we were found out, we'd have been as easy to spot as passion-pink fire engines.

I found her in the lobby, leaning one elbow up against the concession stand and eating popcorn out of a family-sized Buttercup tub.

"Grab some—might be all you get for a while." She jammed the tub into my chest.

"Save it." I was ready to jump down her throat for being so lame. "C'mon, the match is starting. We go now or we forget about it. If you're not up to it, just say so. I can hitch a ride to Crosswell by myself. Might be easier than dragging you along anyway."

"Don't get all hyper. It's all set. See that guy over there?" Heidi rolled her eyes in the direction of the men's room. "That's our ride."

Our ride was a stringbean cowboy freak type all duded

up in faded jeans with a calico patch at each knee and one of those checkered shirts where everything snaps together and the pockets and cuffs are trimmed with curly arrow decorations. He was wearing a ten-gallon number with the rim rolled to a point and a silver band strung together out of beer-can pop-tops. Hair hung down past his shoulders, absolutely radiant. It was the only clean thing about him.

From inside the auditorium a voice bubbled over the microphone and the crowd growled like something in a cave. The match was beginning. I wanted to take a look, but Heidi grabbed me by the sleeve.

"Wait," Heidi said, "he's gonna leave in about two minutes."

The cowboy froze to the wall, jerking his head in our direction. He was wearing aviator shades, the kind with the mirror lenses so there was no telling what he was looking for. The lobby was thinning out fast now that the wrestling was under way.

Suddenly two men brushed right by us, walking in a dead straight line across the floor to the men's room. Both wore varsity football jackets, pale orange with darker orange W's where the letters had been torn off. Washed-up jocks, I figured then, because both men seemed well into their thirties. One had a grocery bag bunched under his arm. He went into the men's room while the other bummed a light off the cowboy and stood there with the cigarette burning down to the filter, pinched between his fingers like a dead bug. As soon as he dropped the butt and stamped it out with his heel, the other guy came out of the bathroom, checking his fly. The bag under his arm seemed to have been crumpled into a brown wad. Both men spun toward us and circled right by us on out the entrance. The cowboy's mouth crinkled into a smirk. He twisted his head in a slow arc from one corner of the lobby to the other, waited a ten count, and disappeared into the men's room.

Another ten count and he was out again, walking right at us with a gym bag in his right hand.

"What's going on anyhow?" I whispered to Heidi. She smashed her popcorn tub into a flat disc and tossed it into a box behind the counter.

"Just hussssshhhh. Do you wanna go or don't you?" The cowboy moseyed over real peaceful like, his boot heels popping on the floor. He walked up to Heidi and rested the bag on the counter.

"Nice work, sugar. This must be the boy, is it?" He twisted his head sideways toward me like maybe I was a bag of laundry. Heidi nodded.

"You drive a Volkswagen, boy?" he asked, still without looking at me.

"Sure."

"Okay. Lime green, New York plates, a Beetle, you know what a Beetle is?"

"Sure," I repeated.

"Good boy. It's in the front lot. Here's the key. Don't screw up."

I found the green bug, no sweat, and was about ready to get in when a roar rattled the windows of the auditorium. The announcer's voice followed, a hollow echo impossible to understand even before it was swamped by a wave of boos. The match was over. The Gator Man was in there— win, lose or draw. Whatever, he had broken in, he had finally gotten his shot at being something more than "ordinary." Now it was up to me, aspiring boy wonder and, like the old man, terminal underachiever, to pull the rest of it together.

I pulled around front where Heidi and the cowboy jumped

in, beating back a flock of kamikaze moths that had clustered in the light under the marquee. The cowboy slid into the backseat and curled up, like a sea horse. His head rested on the gym bag. Heidi sat beside me with her feet hitched up on the dashboard. I got on the first road we hit and turned right, heading anywhere. After about three minutes of squirming in her jeans, Heidi managed to pull out our ragged map of Georgia and a strawberry-flavored Charleston Chew. She bit the end of the wrapper off and spit it out the window. Then she settled back in her seat to study the map with the candy clamped between her teeth.

"Figure maybe a hundred miles. Look for sign that says Atlanta, then head south on Seventy-five."

"No interstates, none of that crap or the deal's off. Those big roads make me, like, carsick, so don't give me no gut ache." The cowboy talked through his nose in a fierce monotone. He didn't sound like any cowboy I'd ever heard. And I didn't think his allergy to interstates was due to any stomach problem, either.

It was getting to be heavy twilight by the time we were out of Macon for good and heading through slash pine forests planted in perfect rows, all straight lines and diagonals whichever way you looked. We came to an intersection of blinking yellow lights. A sign pointing right said "Hester 23," and Heidi said it was our road. She had calculated a route of zigzagging back roads that would take us to Crosswell in about twice the time, but I could settle for that. No hurry, really, because two teenaged kidnappers skulking around the back roads of a red-clay country town after midnight are almost certain to draw attention.

The road led through more pine forests becoming denser with the darkness. We passed no cars until we reached Hester, a town of wooden shacks built for the families who cut the trees or worked in the mills. Beyond, two identical churches stood on either side of the road, and then the gas stations, all dark. After Hester there was nothing. Only the stink of a paper mill hinted there might be someone beyond the trees. Heidi closed her window against the foul air and left it closed. A car approached from behind, the first. It passed us at probably twice our speed without dimming its bright lights.

Adjusting the rearview mirror to escape the glare, I caught a glimpse of the cowboy. His hat had fallen over his face; he seemed asleep. I caught a look at Heidi out of the corner of my eye. She had barely spoken since Macon. What did she know about the cowboy? There was no way we could talk now.

Night driving—just staring into the two cones of light pushing their way along an unknown road—is hypnotic. Funny things happen in those highway trances—over every rise the road ends. Or strange faces, night shapes, jump up out of the blackness and dissolve in the light of your high beams. I held the wheel a little tighter, expecting the next turn to plunge us headlong off the edge.

19

Time flattened out and disappeared. After a while I wasn't sure if it was ten or midnight or three in the morning. Heidi had passed out. She slumped sideways into her seat, breathing in choppy gulps through her mouth. There was no sound from the backseat. The VW engine was winding up, throbbing in fluttery beats like the heart of an overworked hummingbird. It could blow any minute. The suspense was the only thing that kept me awake.

Finally, from out of the dark, a sign lunged its rusty face right at us: "Culpepper Funeral Home—A Tradition of Serving the Families of Eulee Springs Since 1894."

A real town, at last, with dead people and everything! After that the signs came in bunches: "State Farm Insurance," "The First Pentecostal Church," "Omar Perkins for Sheriff," "The High Hat Motel" and "Massey Ferguson," all in a row. The comforts of home. Nothing said how far, but Heidi woke up and said she thought she smelled flowers, and that meant gardens and little old ladies with straw hats and white gloves.

"Better slow it down, ace," the cowboy rasped from the back seat, awake now too. "This place is a snake pit." When I asked what snakes had to do with anything, he described the dangers of driving through Georgia with New York plates.

"Used to have my own set of Georgias," he said, meaning, I suppose, Georgia license plates. "Bastards meaner than ever now that the interstate's taken most of their business away. Go easy."

But it was too late. Two blue points of light came spinning into the rearview mirror. They were a long ways off, but closing fast. I didn't have to say anything; the cowboy knew it already.

"It saddens me to part company so sudden-like. Pull over that next rise, then ease to the side and get out fast. Get down in the ditch and stay there."

The cowboy came over my seat and started squeezing me right over into Heidi. He had the wheel himself and eased over just like he'd told me to do.

"Now out—I ain't stoppin', so roll." Heidi snapped the door open. "Wait, take this, Princess," the cowboy added. He grabbed his crumpled gym bag from the backseat and shoved it into Heidi's arms. "Just watch it for me, honey, and I'll catch up to you like I said. Consider it a promise. *Now go!*" I considered it more of a threat than a promise, but I didn't say so.

As soon as we hit the ditch, the police car whined by above us, then slowed farther on down the road, its siren dying in a throaty growl. We sat frozen in the ditch among the hum of crickets as the woods throbbed in the blue lights of the distant patrol car. Then the light was gone. The woods got dark and stayed that way. Beside me Heidi emptied out her shoulder bag, jammed the gym bag into its bottom, then refilled it.

"Let's go," I whispered to her. I took her arm and we crawled up the embankment and looked around. No trace of anything. We walked cautiously along the roadside, a hundred yards, two hundred yards. No sign of anyone; no cars, no blood, even the gravel seemed undisturbed. We kept on, saying nothing.

No telling how far we walked before, finally, the crickets hushed and the dogs commenced barking. After maybe forty minutes we started passing houses and tumbledown plywood shacks where school kids huddled out of the rain. Then past Rodman's Chicken Kitchen, with a plastic chicken big as a Buick doing 360s on the roof. In another block we passed the Dixie Drive-In with its bug zapper burning away like some killer night-light.

Eulee Springs at, like, four in the morning, was dead to the world. We hurried by the graveyard, past neat white houses looking like they'd all been built the same day, and on into the prosperous inner city. Everything was brick: banks, post office, drugstore, Laundromat, even the sidewalks. We took a turn off the main street, and Heidi removed her wooden sandals—she sounded like one of those shaggy horses looking for its beer truck—and went barefoot. One block back we came to a park, more like a town square, actually, where a wrought-iron fence seemed ready to collapse inward on three sides. Some bronze Rebel soldier stood guard over the park with a musket across his knee and a ring of diseased geraniums at his feet.

We walked through the park and up the three or four steps onto a weathered old bandstand. It must have gone through ten coats of paint, all peeling. The floor was rough, splintered in some places, and from outside the stench of urine, almost to ammonia, wafted through. Heidi winced and held her nose.

"Just close your eyes and pretend it's the Holiday Inn," I said. Heidi smiled and dropped her bag.

"I can if you can" was all she said, and then she lay down at my feet with her bag for a pillow. I joined her. It felt so good just to let my entire weight spread out across those cool boards that it didn't matter if we were nowhere, getting nowhere fast. By then I was ready to simply let it all slide, and sleep till they took me away. I closed my eyes and pulled closer to Heidi, and she curled over into my arms.

"Too tight?" I asked.

"Not tight enough," Heidi answered.

"I suppose things could be worse than this," I said.

"Most things are worse than this," she said. "Now hush."

Then, coiled together in the stale dust, we fell asleep.

I awoke with a boot in my gut. "This here ain't no Los Angy-lees, son. Folks in Eulee Springs frown on vagrants sleeping in Mosely Park. 'Course, we don't get many runaways here, seeing how we're not on any of your major thoroughfares. Better get your girlfriend up, we going for a stroll." I nudged Heidi in her ribs and rolled over on my back to see where the voice was coming from.

He could have been on the PGA tour. He had lemon slacks, a hot-pink knit shirt with golf tees criscrossed on the pocket and one of those pro-shop caps with the ventilated crown. His face was the color of bricks, but he stopped far short of qualifying for a redneck Georgia sheriff. Another dream shattered.

"You Omar Perkins?" I asked, remembering the sign on the way into town.

114

"The very one, that's right. And who would you be?" he replied.

"Nelson Gato, sir," I answered before I had time to realize a phony name might have been better. But then, he had me dead to rights anyway. He shot a hand toward me, and I ducked to one side before I figured out he was only wanting to shake. I took his hand, gave it my best he-man squeeze, and he pulled me up onto my feet.

"My pleasure, Mr. Gato. Now bring your friend along and we'll get you some breakfast."

After Heidi managed to get herself half awake, we followed Sheriff Perkins back toward the main street, where "headquarters" was a little office tucked away at the back corner of the Eulee Springs Credit Union and former part-time CETA agency. The sheriff sat us down and poured us coffees while he went over our IDs. "Nothing unusual," he said. Then he left to get something. I guessed he was probably calling the Macon police to report some missing persons. But instead, he came back with two orders of grits, eggs-to-go and a box of semithawed Sara Lee doughnuts.

"Most important meal of the day," the sheriff said, beaming. He started sucking on a doughnut, defrosting it as he ate. "Now, I think you owe me some explanation as to what brings you to Eulee Springs."

"Yessir, well, you see, glump, glump," I did this routine about choking on my grits until I could think of something halfway convincing to say. "Uh . . . we were . . . that is, we got a ride with this fellow, said he could take us to Hester, and so, you know—"

"Tell the truth now, Nelson," Heidi interrupted. "Truth is, sheriff, we were planning to get married, which is why we ran away from home in Florida. So anyway, we got up

115

here, say, two or three yesterday. Macon, that is, we were in Macon."

"Yessir," I joined in, "that's absolutely accurate, and then this guy up there says we need a blood test. Only he says we got to go to some peoples' clinic, but when we get there—"

"Yeah, so we get there and this nurse with a blond mustache gives us some number about needing birth certificates and then I show her my temporary permit, but all she says is, 'I'm sorry, I'm sorry,' like that's supposed to make it better."

"That's Georgia law these days," the sheriff said. "Nothing you can do about that." He stared into the bottom of his coffee mug.

"Oh, but sheriff, Nelson and I are so truly and deeply in love, it's like these laws are just made up to ruin our lives," Heidi moaned. She scraped her chair across the floor to mine and took my hand to demonstrate the total sincerity of our young love. "Everyone told us to wait until we graduated, but we just *knew* we were doing the right thing. It was like a message from God, the very day my daddy's body rejected a heart transplant. Nelson moved in right across the street and has taken care of me ever since. At first he just helped Mamma with the grass, but then he'd come over for Sunday dinner and change Mamma's oil, and we'd spend nights playing canasta in the breezeway, and then Mamma would read us Scripture. My mamma's a Christian saint in her own right, but when she started making Nelson dress up in Daddy's old pajamas we decided it was time had come to make a few changes in our relationship. Mamma said we were consumed by carnal desires, but like Nelson says, that's just the devil trying to break her heart with godless attributions."

116

"Godless attributions?" The sheriff threw me a puzzled look. I shrugged a silent apology on Heidi's behalf and slouched farther into my chair. Her saga continued, incoherent, until I was convinced she was going to fall on the floor and start speaking in tongues.

". . . and so when I get home one Saturday night with Nelson, Mamma has Reverend Mr. Lucas and half her Temple of Divine Truth Bible study group lying on the kitchen floor praying for my salvation and deliverance from the fires of everlasting damnation. Then the reverend starts laying on his hands to purify my soul, which is when Nelson kicks his butt and chases all the old biddies out like a flock of wet geese. No, make that a gaggle. . . ."

"Make what a gaggle?" the sheriff asked. He took off his golf cap and stroked his crewcut head like he was reading the greens for invisible bumps. A monumental groan escaped from somewhere in my throat, purely involuntary. Sheriff Perkins replaced his cap and I belched. "Misfortune and grits don't mix, son. How about a Tums for the old plumbing?"

I shook my head and Heidi started off stroking the back of my neck. She launched on some new tirade about how my insides are being ravaged by some gastrointestinal disorder. Terminal ulcers, she explained, going on about how some doctor told me they'd claim my life by the time I was thirty. My only hope was acupuncture. We were saving up for a trip to China, where they were working miracles. She had written the President for a loan. *Sixty Minutes* wanted our story. Mike Wallace was interested. And on, and on and on . . .

The sheriff had to excuse himself right then. He just walked outside for air, shaking his head in disbelief.

I grabbed Heidi's hand from around my neck and twisted

117

her until I could see her face. "Are you on something or what?" I hissed at close range. Her pupils looked dilated. She seemed straight. "What a crock, what an absolute crock. You think he's dumb or what? Nobody's that dumb. Nobody. Let him ask the questions. We're not out of here yet. You want to go to the nuthouse? Keep that up and you're as good as in."

"You started it," she smiled. "I was just trying to give it a little flavor."

"Ain't nobody can swallow the flavor you gave it. Where'd you get that story, anyhow?"

"*Eager to Love*," she says, "The continuing story of restless youth torn by love and passion in the raw."

"Very raw," I mumble.

"Weekdays at two-thirty," she added. "Right after *The Healers and the Losers*, which smells ever since Dr. Dunleavy got murdered in Venezuela. The new chief of neurosurgery was going to marry Dr. Dunleavy's widow, but he might be gay, and so she switched over to *Eager to Love* anyway. She's the third Laura Winters they've had in three years. Her ex-husband's got her in court. Wants her declared incompetent so he can have their new baby."

"Really neat. That's enough to give anyone terminal ulcers."

"Oh, it's not terminal ulcers at all. It's stomach cancer. Poor Chad, all the Forresters have such terrible luck. Sherrill just doesn't want Chad to know, at least not until she can have her mother committed. But the church is fighting it. Reverend Lucas is really Sherrill's older brother, but they got put in separate orphanages when they were little, and now Sherrill's mother thinks that Chad and Lucas are—"

"All right, all right, I get the idea, now just drop the whole routine. If we ever get out of here, I'll try to find

118

you a hobby until your head gets untwisted."

"Just mind your own head, which is more twisted than mine'll ever be."

Well, I was about ready to ask for an explanation of that remark when the sheriff walked back in and handed me an envelope full of cash with a pink note stapled to the bills.

"Give that to Mr. Sims at the bus station down the street. He'll put you on a bus for Florida. That should cover it exactly. Now, I don't think I'll have to walk you down there. If you show around here again, we'll have to run you through the blender. You are good folks, if my judgment don't betray me. Don't prove me wrong. Now, tell all your people that Omar Perkins gave you breakfast and tried to do right by you. Hurry on, we only got one bus and it don't wait for God hisself. Now shoo."

"Thank you, Mr. Perkins," I said, trying to grab his hand to show how really grateful I was that he was willing to overlook Heidi's looneytunes monologue. But he shepherded us right out, pushing from behind, hardly giving Heidi time to grab her bag or check her hair for strays.

"Now, you speak kindly of Eulee Springs every chance you get," he hollered down the street behind us. He was hanging out the doorway by one arm and waving with the other. "And, oh, say, hey, young lady," he calls after Heidi. She spins and walks backwards slowly on the brick walk. "Just keep on watchin'. . . . Dollars to doughnuts Laura gets to keep the baby. I'd stake my reputation as a lawman on that."

"Me, too," Heidi calls back and then breaks out into a giggle that lasts her maybe twenty minutes into our bus ride on out of Eulee Springs and down along the flat roads, through sorghum fields and rows of red-dusted peanuts, stretching for miles.

119

20

I congratulated Heidi on finding another member of the *Eager to Love* fan club. According to her, the sheriff was a sweetheart of a guy. I agreed, admitting that he needed a soft spot the size of a rotten honeydew just to swallow all that low-IQ melodrama. I figured Eulee Springs just didn't have enough real sex and violence to keep an honest lawman from going a little soggy in the frontal lobes. Heidi was feeling so positively smug that she smoked most half a pack of her cigarettes and then went into the john to throw up. I knocked on the door and told her I was going up front to try for a chat with the bus driver.

Up front, the bus driver sat in his working grays with stripes down the sides of his pants. He was as gray as his pants and somewhat grainy, like he'd been molded out of prestressed concrete. A transistor radio hanging from the back of the seat was pumping away on country music. Eugene Somebody started singing about all the broken hearts and bottles litterin' up his life: "No return and no deposit, keep your heart locked in the closet, empty dreams and empty bottles thrown away." A sign over the window said "Do *not* talk to the driver," so I just stood there staring out the window until the driver asked if I was wanting to get off in Doraville. I told him I was wanting to get to Crosswell, and he tells me I got the wrong bus and the wrong bus line. Which of course I knew already. He offered me a handful of pistachios and then told me to switch in Bougaville up ahead. All we gotta do is cash in our Gulf Piedmont Motor Tours tickets at the station and catch the Greyhound toward Atlanta. I thanked him for the information and he smiled back real friendly, with little green nut morsels stuck between his teeth.

The station in Doraville was a drugstore with a screen door and eight thousand skin mags snuggled in shrink-wrap. The man at the counter gave us tickets to Crosswell but refused to refund the rest of Sheriff Perkins's money, which is about what I was expecting anyway. By the time our bus showed, we managed to polish off a liter of Pepsi and two Brownie chocolate drinks. Heidi also managed to liberate a box of Junior mints and a jumbo bag of vinegar-flavored potato chips, which she stuck sideways in her bulging shoulder bag. I put a few bad words on her about the sticky-finger routine, but all she did was brag about how smooth she was with cramming all that crinkly paper into her "hiding place" without getting caught. Which I suppose shows some kind of raw aptitude for something.

I started in giving her a sermon about the dangers of associating with undesirable types, like, for instance, our old cowboy friend. She got a little insulted at that. "Highlight of our trip," she said, and started sucking on a mint.

121

By the time we were on the bus and heading back to Cross-well she had gotten tough as leather, then soft as butter, then smooth as custard pudding. First she wanted to score some hash when school started up. Then she wanted to take the day-care class 'cause nobody ever asks her to baby-sit and she's got to start thinking about how to be a good mother. She wants two girls and two boys, preferably in sets of twins—and zero population growth can go to hell if they don't approve. I told her I approve, and she took my hand in her lap, stroking it like it was a pet hamster.

I let my hand seek its own level, so to speak, but by the time I was really warming to my subject, I glanced over to catch Heidi's reaction, only to realize she'd closed her eyes, asleep. She'd zonked, dead gone, and I pulled my hand away to watch her sleep.

Her face softened and the defiant jaw settled into sleep. Soon the sassy teen queen was gone and the girl that was left behind seemed younger—or maybe just not so eager to be old.

Finally, two hours later, Heidi woke up with a jolt and lit right into me with her patented razor tongue: "Jeezem, you'da let me sleep through the whole friggin' ride and I'd wake up tomorrow in Philadelphia or some damn place. If I had to depend on you . . . God, what a numb-numb you can be. Say, what? We're here?"

While the bus idled at the curb right alongside the Cross-well Consumers Savings Bank, I stood up and stretched, fighting back a yawn. This was our stop. Heidi unfolded her long legs from underneath the seat in front of her and stood up, too.

I pulled her down the aisle behind me to the front door. There was a sign in the stairwell: "Please watch your step." As I paused long enough to focus my bleary eyes on the

122

letters, Heidi walked practically right up my back. We spilled down the steps and landed like a pile of wrinkled laundry. Heidi sat on top of me until I rolled over and left her sprawling on the scorching sidewalk.

21

By the time Heidi caught up with me, I was jammed inside
the phone booth checking Ruthie's address in the yellow
pages. There it was, Ruthie's Hair Designs, even featured
in a one-eighth-page block ad with some foxy Greek-type
goddess leaning against a Corinthian column, her hair stirred
up into a froth of little ringlets. The address was the same,
37 Cheesman Road.

"Gonna call or what?" Heidi asked, kicking in the folding
door. She was dipping into her bag of vinegar chips and
pointed the open top into my face—a little peace offering.

"Naw, you're gonna call. Make an appointment. Here's
the dime," I said, flipping her the coin. "And leave the
door open. It's like a microwave in there."

She handed me the chips, and I stood outside while she
called. My T-shirt was sweat-soaked and sticking to my
back. After three tries, Heidi discovered it was a dial-now-

pay-later-type phone. Finally she got through, mumbled into the receiver and hung up.

"You think I'd look good with short hair? Maybe something curly? Might look good with my earrings, huh, Nelson?" She came grinning out of the booth and reclaimed her bag of chips.

"So what happened, who'd you talk to?" I asked.

"Just some nice lady, said she had a cancellation and could take me at three-thirty. Isn't that lucky? I'm getting a shampoo, a cut and a set. I just hope she don't ruin me."

"Right, look, who'd you talk to? Did she have sort of a squeaky little accent, or was it just an everyday kind of voice?"

"Wasn't squeaky, no, but Lord, how'm I supposed to know what kind of voice? All she said was, 'Thank you so very much for calling.' "

Thank you so very much. Always the same, the exact same, whether she'd be getting change at the supermarket or a ticket from the toll collector on the Skyway Bridge. Thank you so very much, just like that. Mom had a hundred ways of letting people know she was what she liked to call a "civilized lady." She wore dresses for downtown even in the heat, and never smoked on buses or at restaurants, and begged just about everyone's pardon at the slightest bump. Dad kidded her once about going to finishing school and majoring in etiquette, but it was never quite as faky as all that. Just a habit, like the fancy way she crossed the *t* in Gato.

"That's her, that's my mom," I said. "Now, all we gotta do is find Cheesman Road. Did she say anything about how to get there?"

"Wouldn't that be dumb. She'd know right off we weren't from Crosswell. Let's start walking. This place makes Eulee

125

Springs look like urban blight. It can't be that far."

Heidi checked the coin return for spare change and, finding none, slammed the phone booth door behind her and joined me on the sidewalk. We headed back in the direction of the drugstore–bus station and kept on right through town, checking every side street for road signs. Nothing looked even close. It was getting on toward three, and the town was thinning out, the houses coming farther apart and set back off from the road in among clumps of pine and azalea bushes. Crosswell was looking all used up when we came to Nadeau's Night Owl, a down-and-out gas station disguised as an all-night variety store. A sign over the door said "Nadine Nadeau, Prop.," and we went inside for a word with Nadine.

"What can I do y'all for?" Nadine asked from behind a counter stocked with pickled eggs and Slim Jims. She was wearing a pink sleeveless sweater stretched over these two all-purpose breasts, pointing off at angles like a pair of Maidenform torpedoes. A chain of simulated pearls slid down between the twin peaks and dangled a small loop in midair just over the summits. Her hair was white, but her face was as taut and golden as a well-baked pie.

"Yes, ma'am, we're trying to find Cheesman Road, but I think we must of got twisted around," I tell her in my best Georgia accent. "My girlfriend's gettin' her hair fixed up for a wedding, you see."

"Ruthie's, she's a doll that Ruthie, does all my girls' hair until you couldn't tell 'em from angels on high. See here—" and she produces a handbill from under the counter. "Nadine's School of Baton and Acrobatic Dance" it says, and there's a picture of twelve little girls with bodies like two-by-fours, all standing with one leg cocked and one arm raised in a baton salute. The girls seem mostly nine, ten,

126

eleven, just like that, except for their hair. The hair is all platinum and honey blond, piled in twists and curls and French cascades like the fancy ladies' 'dos in some *Modern Man* yearbook.

"They're darlings, every last one of them, precious things."

"Yessum, I can see that. . . ."

"This here third girl is Chandra Cheesman, named Chandra Lane after her, you'll see it on your way. She's such a sweet thing you'd never know her daddy's just plain rolling in it."

"No, ma'am, you wouldn't," I agreed. "Now, uh, about Cheesman Road?"

"Just keep on like you're going, hon. About half a mile out, you'll come to a big sign that says Oak Terrace Estates. Road going in there loops around, so's you can't miss it. Old Chuck Cheesman built up all around out there, practically stole that land from the U.S. government, but they're so ignorant anyways."

I round up Heidi from behind a shelf of fruit-pie snacks, and we start out.

"By the way, hon," Nadine calls out behind us. I pause in the doorway. "Your girlfriend a twirler?"

"No, ma'am, not a twirler."

"Too bad, she carries herself like a twirler. See how she prances?"

"Yes, ma'am."

"And you tell Miss Ruthie howdy-do from Nadine—she'll know who . . ."

"Yessum, bye-bye."

22

So me and Heidi proceeded in a southerly direction, keeping to the right side of the road, where all the shade seemed to congregate. Nadine said another half mile, but it felt like ten times that, all the same. The only air moving seemed to lift off the steamy tarmac in transparent waves thick and stale as dog's breath. Heidi trudged ahead of me with her head bent, measuring her steps along the road's edge. I slowed to match her rhythm, three paces behind. No use rushing, and no use talking, either, for now. Walking was enough.

Finally, we got to the entrance to Oak Terrace Estates. We collapsed in a rectangle of shade under the big rough pine sign and spread out on our backs in a patch of dry-roasted joe-pye weed.

"Here, try these on. It's your undercover disguise." Heidi pulled something out of her bag. Sunglasses—wraparound, no less—with polarized lenses, according to the square silver tag still attached to one stem. "Whenever you're ready," she said, jumping to her feet. Her back was plastered with dead leaves and twigs, sticking to her sweat-soaked blouse.

I stood up beside her and brushed the debris off. "There, you're almost ravishing. C'mon, I'll follow you up until we find the house. You go in and get your hair chopped off or whatever. Get talking to my mom. She'll be the good-looking one with my nose." I shot her my profile while she memorized my nose.

"Poor thing," Heidi said.

"Tell her you baby-sit. Ask her if she's got kids. You know, like, 'Oh, a little girl, I just bet she's adorable. Is she around? I'd just love to see her,' and if she's not, find out where she is. If you don't get Mom, then ask for a manicure. She does nails, I think."

"Right, and what are you going to do while I'm pumping your mother?"

"Depends on what you find out. I gotta sneak us some wheels. Mom's Chevy'll do if it's available. Watch for me when you get out."

"Where?"

"Just watch for me. If you don't see me right off, come on back down here. If I'm not here, just keep walking back to town."

Heidi pondered on that for a while. Never mind that the whole scheme was half-baked, the important thing was to act like you knew what was coming off, even if you didn't. And I didn't.

A tunnel of drowsy pines bent over the road as we walked up the slope toward the neat rows of development homes. The whole deal was like a grander version of Gate o' Palms,

129

with pines for palms and houses for trailers. Right then I was thinking how much easier it would have been to be back home, parked in front of the silver tube catching up on a rerun of *Star Trek* and swilling down a liter bottle of RC Cola.

Easier, maybe, but boring. After all, there was Heidi, half-crazy and just a tad delirious, but ready for anything, a real smorgasbord of earthly delights. Somehow her appetite for weirdness had rubbed off on me.

We passed Chandra Lane, as predicted, then Ginger Way and Luellen Street before we finally came upon Cheesman Road. I checked my wallet and pulled out a bill from the General's slush fund. I pressed the ten into Heidi's palm.

"Okay, now let's don't blow it. If it gets tense, just clam up and leave when you're finished."

"Relax, Nelson, I haven't screwed up yet." She seemed to mean it, so I let that pass. No time to destroy morale. Then Heidi grabbed me around the neck and pulled me to her for a quick "smack" right on the lips.

"There's one to grow on," she said. "Now, don't run off."

It was a salty kiss. I realized how wasted she looked. Her face was glazed with a layer of sweat and dust. If Ruthie didn't throw her out right off, or strip her and hose her down, it would be a miracle. The corners of her eyes were packed with small crumbs of dirt. Her neck was streaked with a gray smudge that could have passed for shadow in bad light. Still, she was beautiful in a grimy kind of way. I had a feeling then like I wanted to protect her, or even rescue her from something. Only problem was, I didn't know from what.

Heidi strutted on up Cheesman Road like she'd just gotten her second wind. It was going on two days now since she'd seen a bed, but she could still motivate like a spring-driven thing. What a marvel from behind! Her backside twitched and rolled in perfect time while her bag swung from her shoulder, slapping against her hip at every other beat. Well, I mean she was humming down that road. I swear I don't know where she got it.

She reached the driveway of a sand-yellow house with a wrought-iron lamppost at the end and turned in without hesitating. It must have been Ruthie's. From where I was standing the house angled away from my view. Heidi disappeared around its corner and was gone. I figured it would be half an hour at least before she'd reappear. Time enough for a little reconnaissance.

The houses were sealed tight against the sweltering afternoon, curtains drawn, everyone inside probably sipping away at iced tea. I slipped along from one backyard to the next, reading meters as I went, just in case anyone was watching.

Finally, I got to the far corner, where I could look Ruthie's garage right in the eye. There was the old Chevy, pointing out—ideal. Not a creature was stirring. I crossed, slow and deliberate, and hunkered behind the passenger side of the car. Still no sound. Vanessa's sand pail sat on the floor, crammed full of old doughnut bags and complimentary catsup from Somebody's Big Boy. More drive-in trash in the back: napkins, straws and Styrofoam hamburger boxes—just like old times.

Old times—funny how the dumbest stuff stuck with you. Like all those Saturday lunches when we'd cash in our two-for-one burger coupons. Vanessa would instantly hand over her pickles, then scrape the onions off with the lid to her soft drink. And Mom, no lie, would pull out her nail clippers and trim the corners off those little catsup packets. And

131

she'd squirrel away the extra napkins for when we got colds and the burger boxes for marigold seedlings the year she decided to have a garden. That stuff always got me crazy, your own family making such a deal out of all those creepy little things. God, how I missed them.

I walked to the door, maybe just to sneak a peek at Mom, a quick fix to keep me going. But no, the red-and-white froufrou curtains were airtight, peekproof, not even dim figures floating back there—nothing. A strange panic got to me. I had forgotten what she looked like, her face, her eyes, her hair, her smile. Did she smile? I tried to remember a dress, anything to get me started, but the curtains filled my eyes, blocking out memory. Was it possible? In another minute I would blast through the door and . . .

I rested my cheek across my forearms, my head tilted out toward the drive. I would have a clear shot of her feet. I waited, one ear tuned to the door behind. Just when I thought I had it under control, my eyelids sagged, dragging me into dreamland. I was going, and didn't nothing matter then. Being stretched out there in the ooze under our old Chevy was the next best thing to being home.

No sooner am I asleep when from somewhere the scraping and popping of wooden soles on concrete comes into my ear. My eyes snap open.

"Pssssssttttt, over here," I hiss. Heidi strolls in my direction, real nonchalant, then spills a pack of her brown cigarettes about ten feet in front of my face. They roll in all directions like crayons. She stoops to pick them up one by one.

"That you, Nelse?" she asks.

"Yeah, 'course it's me. What'd you find out?"

"You were right about your mother—she does nails, see?"

132

She waggles ten chocolate-brown fingernails in my direction.

"They're gorgeous. Where's Vanessa?"

"Calgary Baptist Temple. It's some vacation Bible school back in town."

"Bible school, that figures. Well, take off. I'll give you ten minutes to make the main road. Then we have a reunion. Now hurry." Heidi tucked the last of her cigarettes into their pack, then pulled one out, lit up and was gone. A plume of smoke trailed behind her down the driveway.

My key took a little coaxing but finally turned in the ignition until the accessory light came on and the steering wheel unlocked. I shifted the gear into neutral and turned the wheels to follow the light curving out of the drive. They began to roll, grinding inch by inch across the popping grit underneath. The tailpipe rattled until I eased the gear into drive and let the old Chevy pull itself out of the garage and down to Cheesman Road.

I kept my eye on the house. No door opened, no curtain ruffled at the window. Tight as a clam. I had pulled it off.

When I caught up with Heidi, she was maybe halfway down the road to the main entrance. I eased over to let her in. She slammed down on the front seat and slid across beside me.

"Tell me I'm not something now, c'mon and tell me that," she looped an arm around my neck and twisted my head around till I was looking at her straight on.

"You're somethin', for sure. Now, if we can just find a big-enough jar of formaldehyde . . ." At that, she began to mutilate my face with her chocolate fingernails.

"Creep, you couldn't appreciate true feminine beauty if your life depended on it."

"Maybe it does," I said, finally taking hold of both her wrists to keep her from raking me across the eyeballs. She was really looking fine, once I took a solid look. Her long hair had been chopped off, leaving a sort of dark, bristly bonnet. You could see her face, her neck, even the hoops of her hypoallergenic earrings. She looked older and younger both at the same time.

"Okay, the truth is you look really fine. I'm sorry I'm a lunt sometimes."

"Hairdo magic, a butterfly is born," Heidi was posing herself in the rearview mirror and sucking in her cheeks like all those scrawny high-fashion types on the cover of *Vogue*. Mom always said they got that way from swallowing tapeworms.

"How much for all that?" I asked. We were coming into Crosswell, but still no churches.

"All of it," Heidi answered.

"Ten bucks! I mean you're ravishing and all that, but jeez."

"Shampoo, cut, style, that's about right. And don't forget your mother did my nails. And I had to leave a tip."

"A tip? You tipped my *mother*!"

"She was nice. She really does good nails, too."

"What did she say?"

"Not much. I had to squeeze the Bible school thing out of her."

"Squeeze how?" I asked.

"Oh, nothing fancy. Just started telling her about my sister Vanetta, and she said how that was almost like a coincidence 'cause she had a sweet little girl name of Vanessa, and I said, really?, and how I'd like to see her and she says, too bad but Vanessa's at vacation Bible school, and I say, down at New Life Holiness?, and she says, no, at Calgary Baptist."

"How'd she seem?"

"Oh, sad, maybe. Course, maybe I was looking for that. She did sigh a lot. Or she had a cold, that could have done it. You know how you breathe through your mouth when you're stuffy."

"Sure. Anything else?"

"Not really. Just that you do have her nose—only bigger, of course."

"Of course," I said, touching my nose for any trace of Mom's that I could remember, and feeling fairly sad myself.

23

A second look at Crosswell didn't change it much. A roadside dairy stand was filling up with late-afternoon customers. On top, a ten-foot cone rose, weathered and orange, like it was announcing a new flavor breakthrough, rust ripple. Farther on, the same feed store, the same banks and drugstores stood baking like giant brick potatoes. It was hot, is my point. Not much going, and still no churches. We circled off the main street, making a loop at every block. After about three passes into downtown Crosswell we started easing into suburbia again. Our fourth block turned up a United Brethren something or other, and a Zion House of Worship with a marquee reading "Jam with the Savior—Sunday Morning Fever Will Get Your Soul."

Our next block was pay dirt. The Calgary Baptist Temple was your basic Georgia brick, right out of a Lionel train set, with its nifty white double doors and a steeple with a gold cross up top. There were even authentic pigeons sitting in small bunches on each eave, heads bowed and prayerful, chortling out little hymns. Behind the church was a freshly paved parking lot lined with giant live oaks on two sides. We pulled into the lot and around back, where a small patch of worn grass was disguised as a playground. A pack of kids, all barefoot and brown, scrabbled around in the dirt. None of them had Bibles that I could see.

Heidi hunched herself up to the dashboard. "Bet anything I can pick her out." She studies the action for a while then announces, "There, the little scrawny one sitting on that boy's legs."

"No way," I tell her, squinting at the two kids tangled up in their own private cloud of dust. "Besides, that's a boy, they're both boys. Matter of fact, I don't see Vanessa anywhere. You sure this is the right church?"

"Course it is. How many Calgary temples you think they got here in Crosswell, Georgia, anyways?" She sat back and lit a cigarette. "Probably she could be inside weaving pot holders or praying or whatever they do—see, there's some." Four kids came tear-assing out the back door to join the others. But still no Vanessa.

I left Heidi in the car and walked across to the edge of the playground where the two boys had managed to switch positions in the dirt. "Do any of you guys know Vanessa Gato? She's supposed to be around here somewheres."

"Sure, we know Ratface Gato. Who are you?" The kid stared at me while he blew his nose on the edge of his T-shirt.

"I'm her brother. I'm looking for her to take home."

"Oh, she's got a brother," the kid said, half to himself. Then, "That 'Ratface' don't mean nothing, you see, it's just like a name we call her. We all got nicknames, you see,

137

it's just like a name we call her. We all got nicknames, just for fun, like."

"Uh-huh, and what's yours?" I asked.

"Spot," the kid shoots back at me like it's a dare. The kid underneath Spot turns his face into the dirt and starts giggling. Wise-ass kids.

"Good, Spot," I say. "Why don't you and Rover go find her for me. Just tell her it's a surprise. Now go fetch." They scuff their way obediently into the back door and after maybe a minute Spot returns by himself.

"Mrs. Ohlmeyer says for you to go inside," the kid reports.

"Come in, come in, we're all in here," a woman's deep soprano voice booms at me. I turn and shrug toward Heidi so she'll know to be a little patient. I stumble my way into the back door, carefully, so as not to step on any kids.

The church is enormous, dark and cool, with the smell of floor wax and old varnish mixing together. When my eyes adjust to the light, I can see Mrs. Ohlmeyer, an extra-stout individual, but incredibly groomed and powdered. Her eyes seem held open by springs, and her smile glows like wax.

"We're having treats today. Won't you join us? The girls made some pecan sandies, and there's spritz cookies and lime-sherbet punch. Won't you have a napkin?"

I shook my head and patted my gut, like I was all full up already. I said I was really just interested in seeing my sister, since we had been having "separate vacations" for most of the summer. And my mom thought maybe it would be fun to sort of surprise old Vanessa, if you catch my meaning. Mrs. Ohlmeyer still looked a little skeptical, so I shot her a wink. That did it.

She rumbled off across the floor to a row of tables. The

girls all clustered around her buzzing together for a minute. Finally they broke their huddle, and scurried off in all directions. "He's good-looking for a brother," one of them squeaked, and the rest busted into giggles and then disappeared altogether.

Mrs. Ohlmeyer held her ground. "The girls will get her. I think she's in the kitchen."

"Yes'm," I mumbled, stuffing my hands into the back pockets of my jeans. Sure enough, from a door at the far corner a familiar stick figure of a girl emerged—then slid backwards through the door as if pulled by elastic. Mrs. Ohlmeyer snorted. Again the figure appeared, this time with a chubby friend in tow.

"Nelson Gato, whatever are you doing here?" she called out.

"Come to see you, Miss Priss. Now get over here," I teased her. With that Vanessa flat flew across the big hall to where I was waiting. She held a big wooden spoon in front of her, waving it like a baton. She reached me, just waist-high, and latched on *thunk*. The spoon digging into my back was cold and sticky.

"Ease up, Vanessa, it's just your old Bubba," I said, reaching back for an old nickname she hadn't used since she was four. Matter of fact, I used to slug her for calling me that very thing.

"You comin' to stay with me and Mamma now? We been missing you sometimes. Everybody here's got brothers and sisters. They think I'm some creepy only child. They think I made you up. Mamma says it's just natural that a boy should stay with his father. Daddy outside? Where is he, is he outside? You gonna live with us now? School starts up another week and a half. You'd like it—they're the Crusaders, it's all brick with a swimming pool and they got a wrestling team, 'cause Chandra's brother's on it and . . ."

"Slow down, hon." I tried to pull her off me long enough to grab the spoon. "What's this mess for?" I asked, holding the spoon at arm's length. It dripped some green goo on the floor.

"Oh, we was just smushing the sherbet into the punch, me and Chandra." She nodded in the direction of the chubby blonde who sidled up to us. Slipping the spoon from my hand, she ran it back across the floor to Mrs. Ohlmeyer, with her hand cupped underneath to catch the green drips. She licked her hand, then reached up and smeared the rest across her chest. Mrs. Ohlmeyer snorted and licked the spoon.

I knelt down to eye level and cupped Vanessa's hands in mine. Her thumbnails were chewed down to the nubs. The flesh was pink and swollen. "Come with me, now," I tried to whisper. "No, Daddy's not outside, he's working hard for us now, though. I got a friend from back home out there, and she'd like to meet you. We came to surprise you. I just wanted to see you—and Mom, of course. Mom let us borrow her car. Now come on. Go tell Mrs. Ohlmeyer it's all right and everything. Tell her I'm your brother and it's okay." And then I gave her a kiss on the nose, but missed as she pulled away to check out with Mrs. Ohlmeyer.

Chandra caught up with my sister halfway across the floor and escorted her to where the large woman stood. Her face knitted into a scowl when Vanessa started her appeal. Chandra refereed. Mrs. O. folded her arms, clenching the spoon in her fist. She looked like the Queen of Hearts. The scowl softened, finally, and Mrs. O. nodded in my direction.

"I suppose it's okay, young man," she boomed in the hollow room, "but you make sure these girls get right home.

This is against our policy, you know. We usually require a note or some call from the parents involved if a change of plan occurs."

"Yes'm, I can understand. We just wanted this to be a surprise, like I said." The girls flew at me, half skipping, and Vanessa caught my arm and started pulling me toward the door.

"Well, a surprise might be one fine thing, but I've still got my punch to blend up, no thanks to you. . . . Well, go on," Mrs. O. called in a final gasp as she pointed the handle of the spoon in the direction of my head. "God bless you anyways. Bango." And I swear I saw the spoon recoil in her hand, the blessing zapped across the empty church and hit me dead center between the eyes.

By the time I snaked my way around the kids and got to the parking lot, Vanessa and Chandra were already settled in the backseat. Only one thing was wrong—I'd come for Vanessa, and got her and a spare in the bargain. This Chandra kid had somehow latched on to our little adventure.

24

When I got to the car I could see things were not exactly going to be one big family picnic. I was hardly behind the wheel when Vanessa starts with the questions.

"What are you Nelson's friend for, anyways?" she asks Heidi point-blank.

" 'Cause we are. Your brother saved me once from a guy who was hassling with me. We just been hangin' out, that's all."

"But Nelson never has girlfriends. Are you his girlfriend, or what?"

"No, we just . . . get along, kinda," Heidi answered.

"That's right, we understand each other," I added. "Doesn't always have to be Ken and Barbie. You'll see, maybe, some-day."

"Oh, brother, whatta crock," Chandra moaned.

"Does Mom know about her yet?" Vanessa asked, nudg-

142

ing me from behind. I pulled out of the parking lot, trying to avoid the question.

"I think she's on drugs," Chandra hissed to Vanessa. "Look at those earrings. They all wear earrings."

"Who does?" Heidi snaps.

"Drug addicts, like on TV."

"Really, and that makes me a drug addict?"

"Well, maybe it does."

"Yeah, well maybe you're a dwarf," Heidi growls.

"Takes one to know one," Chandra taunts through her nose. She and Vanessa collapse on the backseat in a convulsion of tittering. Heidi gives me a look, like I can feel it burning in the side of my neck. I know what she's thinking—get rid of the tagalong.

"Uh, Vanessa hon', why don't you tell me where your friend Chandra lives and we can drop her off first."

"Hollywood, California," Vanessa answers.

"Don't crap around, Vanessa!"

"Really, Nelson, Chandra lives in Hollywood, don't you, Chandra?"

Chandra nods obediently. "Well, it's really El Segundo, but Vanessa thinks Hollywood sounds more romantic."

"Chandra's staying with me and Mom and Aunt Ruthie while her mother and father are in Europe and Paris, all those places," Vanessa explains. "They're really from here, but Aunt Ruthie says after Mr. Cheesman built Oak Terrace all up he moved to California so's he could build shopping centers."

"And condo-mumo," Chandra piped up.

"You mean condominiums, like big apartments where people live all in one building?" I hear Chandra grunt a little "yeah" from the backseat. I began clicking off things I had just heard, and things Nadine at the roadside store had told us. . . . Cheesman . . . big developer . . . owned Crosswell and maybe half of Georgia . . . California shopping centers, condominiums . . . sounded like big money . . . Europe and Paris . . . And Chandra Cheesman was sitting in the backseat, probably worth more than the tomb of King Tut, giggling with my sister and ready to break out in prickly heat. Headlines flashed through my mind: "Developer's Daughter Abducted . . . Shopping-Center Heiress Spirited Away from Bible School . . . Chessman Kidnappers Held by FBI."

Since none of my career objectives included star billing on the Ten Most Wanted list, I concluded that the sooner we dumped Chandra Cheesman, the better.

I could see the clump of trees ahead where the big wooden sign announced the entrance to Oak Terrace Estates. Just pull over, I figured, and tell the kid this is as far as she goes. Let her work it out, waddle her way up to Aunt Ruthie's and tell everything she knows about Vanessa's brother and the dope-crazed girl with the earrings.

"Why we stoppin' here?" Vanessa asks.

"Chandra gets out here," I said, nudging Heidi to open the door on her side. Chandra sits back like she was screwed to the seat.

"No way am I leaving without Vanessa," Chandra announces.

"Me neither," Vanessa says, with a trace of a whine sliding into her voice. I was ready to pound them both into little biodegradable lumps.

"Puky little brats," Heidi explodes, "*this* ain't no Bible school. Do what he says or we'll throw you both in the river."

"What river? No river around here, smartface," Chandra hisses back, right in Heidi's face.

144

Heidi cocked her arm to swat the kid across the chops, but I caught her by the crook of her elbow. I threw the car in reverse. The hell with it. I was ready to back up and turn into the street leading right up to Aunt Ruthie's. Drop Vanessa and snippy little friend at the front door, deposit the car safely back in the garage, and throw myself on the mercy of my mother. And Heidi could lump it if she disapproved.

As soon as the Chevy was back on the asphalt I put her in drive, whipped the wheel hard right, and started to head the car right into Oak Terrace. Then what I saw next made my arm freeze up, locked on that steering wheel and holding her tight until we'd done a 360 and were heading back out on the road and on out of town.

It must have been years of conditioning, training and hardcore guilt, or maybe I just remember what the Gator Man always said: "Po-leece got a name for everything you do, and it'd always come to the same thing—T-R-O-U-B-L-E."

The thing is, when I saw that old bubble-top cruiser gliding down at us like a shark, some strange little fuse inside my brain went *pfffft*. I humped that old Chevrolet full throttle on out of scenic little Crosswell, Georgia. The cruiser was coming our way, but if he was coming after us he wasn't trying all that hard. In another minute he was gone like a cool breeze in August.

"What's the big deal?" Vanessa complained. "Where we going anyhow?"

"Tell you when we get there. Let it be a surprise," I answered. Kids like surprises, I figured, and wherever we ended up, it could sure enough be a surprise.

Suddenly we were playing Twenty Questions.

"Does it have rides, does it have a famous mouse who poses for pictures?" Vanessa asks.

145

"And a Jungle Cruise and teacups that spin?" adds Chandra.

And before I can even get out a word, Heidi throws in a big fat juicy "maybe," and just like that the girls are back there squealing "Disney World, Disney World."

"Hold on now a minute," I begin in protest, but it's no use. Even Heidi has joined in the chant.

"I get to ride next to Nelson on the Space Mountain," Chandra announces. That did it.

"Wooooooo, Nelson, Half Nelson, take me on a ride," Heidi wails in a nasal falsetto.

I throw her a jab with my elbow and miss.

Next, up comes Vanessa. "Chandra's got a crush and it makes her wanta blush. Chandra's got a crrrrrrrr—"

"So just shut up," Chandra threatens through clenched teeth while Heidi, beside me, lights up the front seat with a luminescent smirk.

Me, I just keep my eyes on the road.

25

We drove all that night, me and Heidi taking turns at the wheel. The girls slept in the backseat. I got about four or five hours myself, slumped against the door. It was only a kind of half-sleep though, because every so often we'd veer off the road or screech to a sudden stop in the middle of nowhere. Seems that Heidi kept seeing things. Especially possums. She hated like anything to think about running over possums. It had something to do with them all being mothers and having a pouch full of little blind babies slung underneath their bellies. Of course, you were always seeing them squashed alongside the road anyways. Dad told me it was because they had bad eyes and were kind of sluggish. Plus they weren't too smart, from what I could see.

Still, it was kind of a pain if you were trying to sleep, which is hard enough to do in a car anyways. I told Heidi I was going to get her one of those "I brake for animals" bumper stickers first chance I got. She didn't even smile at that one. In fact, she shut right up and ignored me until there wasn't anything I could do but slump down one more time and pass out.

It was on about the seventy-seventh possum stop that finally two things hit me at the same time. First, the black sky was getting a little diluted with sunlight, especially through the window on Heidi's side of the car. It just got paler and paler until you could see the outlines of clouds somewhere way off over the Atlantic. Then the outlines turned into real clouds, first pink, then kind of tangerine-orange and so on until it was really morning. I hadn't been up this early since the day Mom and Vanessa took off for Georgia in the rain.

The second thing was that we were in Florida. The white herons wading up to their kneecaps in the drainage ditches alongside the road gave it away first. They were always there, digging for frogs or crayfish, just like they'd been paid by the state tourist board to pose for Yankees. And the palmetto clumps gave it away, and the scrub pines and the Spanish moss. But most of all it was just the air, thick and still and filling up with morning sounds like water over a low heat coming to a boil. Just waiting. And of course the highway signs with their outline of the state gave it away, too.

"You awake?" Heidi yawned from across the seat.

"Yeah, almost. Want me to take over?"

"Let's stop first, get some breakfast. The kids need to eat."

We pulled off ten minutes later at a place called Curley's Buck and Bass, a sort of hunting camp, bait shop and restaurant all in one. It was painted all khaki green and beige, like some old German tank from the Black Forest. We filled

148

up on eggs, sausage and biscuits with honey while the girls got sticky with pancakes. They wanted to know when we'd get to Disney World.

"Depends," I told them.

"On what?" Vanessa asked.

"On a lotta things," I said. "On the variables of the situation."

"Means he doesn't know what's going on," Chandra offered between pancakes.

I decided to own up. "So all right. It's a sort of pretend game, what Heidi and I are playing. Like Fantasy World at the Magic Kingdom. Things can seem real even if they're not. We're pretending that you've been kidnapped. If it looks real enough, Mom and Dad will have to . . . like, rescue us. Maybe it'll force us all back together. At least it should let 'em know we want to be. See?"

"Maybe," Vanessa said. "But Mom doesn't really know you got the car, does she? She doesn't even know you were in Crosswell, does she? Well, does she?" I shook my head. "See, she's got no clue, she'll be worried sick."

"Worried sick is what we're going for, honey," Heidi said. "Maybe it'll make all the reasons she left seem suddenly dumb. Rethink her priorities, know what I mean?"

"I do," blurted Chandra, borderline ecstatic. "Cool out, a kidnapping. Wait'll they hear this one back in El Segundo."

"So what's next?" Vanessa asked.

"Who cares?" said Chandra. "As long as they don't tie us up or feed us rice. As long as we get to Disney World."

"What's next, Vanessa," I said, "is I pay the bill and we get out of here. Now finish up and let's go."

After Curley's I drove for a while. It was still pretty early, but the traffic was thickening up. We passed logging trucks, melon trucks, trucks filled with chickens in boxes and some with pigs behind bars. When we came to a city called Chiefland, it looked like the stores were opening up finally, so we pulled into a TG&Y. I gave Vanessa $5.00 to buy some envelopes, scissors, paste and a tablet of Big Chief art paper. She came back with a Strawberry Shortcake stationery set of pink paper and flavored envelopes. They were fine by me, but maybe a little wimpy for kidnap ransom notes.

Heidi bought two newspapers and once we were under way again she started snipping out letters and words. Her theory was that good kidnappers always concealed their identities with cutout notes. I told her it was a good plan for a movie or like that—but I thought we were *wanting* to get caught so as to disgrace our respective parental units into a reconciliation. She said that might work for me, but her daddy was long gone and her mama had nobody to reconcile with. She reminded me that she was just along for the ride and the fine touches. "Creative consultant" is what she called herself.

After maybe twenty more minutes of cutting and pasting Heidi pushed the final product in my face. I hooked it under my thumbs against the steering wheel and read it with one eye, keeping the other eye on the road.

we have the Girls. they are safe. If you want them back, do as you are told. No Police No Goons. we will Contack you on how to do it. Be Smart or the Girls are dumed. ——— thanks
Desperate people

I told her to fix the "Contack" and "dumed." The death threat was stretching it a little bit, but she felt it was part of the style of a good kidnapping note.

She fiddled with the note a little longer and got ready to seal it up. "Hey, what about proof?" she asked.

"Proof of what?"

"You know, proof that we got 'em. Something so they'll know we're serious. Like how they cut off people's ears and things to send in with ransom demands. Real class, if you ask me."

"Sounds kinda nasty."

"Nelson, you're such a dud. It doesn't have to be ears. It could be a tape recording. Remember that movie about Patty Hearst?"

I told her I didn't and besides, we didn't have a tape recorder.

"Hair, that's it, we can send hair." Heidi swiveled around to the girls. "Hey, y'all wanna send a lock of hair?"

"You doing it?" Vanessa asked Chandra.

"Sure I'm doing it," Chandra says, taking the scissors from Heidi, pulling one of her short blond curls from behind her ear and snipping it right off. That convinced Vanessa.

Heidi slipped the hair into the envelope, sealed it and addressed it to Aunt Ruthie. She remembered everything but the zip code.

Then we located the Chiefland post office. I bought a stamp and stuck it on the envelope, and dropped the letter in the "out of town" mail slot. We were in business at last!

Back on the road once more and cruising by Tampa. Then *poof* and it comes to me all at once, just like that—Cactus Territory, the perfect place if it still exists. It was just some junky tourist place for kids, like desert town built on the old highway from Wauchula to Lakeland. Before that it was some defunct go-cart track, and before that it was a trampoline place where you paid a dollar and bounced for an hour. At least that's what Dad said it was, 'cause that was even before my time. Before that I don't know what it was. Except whatever it was, it kept going bankrupt. Probably it was because the old highway didn't get much business once the interstate was finished, so when Cactus Territory finally went under, it went for good. Kind of a ghost town on an old ghost road.

The problem was finding it. I curled east toward Lakeland and then took every road possible south from there. Finally, I hit the one that looked likeliest.

Heidi had passed out again, and the girls were eating oranges and getting sticky one more time. They were getting so stoked up on orange-peel art that they hadn't asked me about Disney World in over an hour. Vanessa had a peel in her mouth covering her teeth. She growled and curled her lips, baring a solid orange grimace.

"Ooohhh, gross me out, you're a werewolf with orange fangs," Chandra squealed as Vanessa growled through her peel. Then it was Chandra's turn. She put a small oval of peel over each eye, like some technicolor Phantom of the Opera. Vanessa giggled and spit her peel into the front seat. Some fun!

Finally, I could see Cactus Territory looming out of the thick growth of trees a little farther down the road. I slowed to scope it out but didn't say "boo," just cruised on by. The place looked like a shipwreck in the middle of a jungle. The old wood buildings—stage depot, bank, saloon, general store—were bleached gray-white from years of sun and rain. They tilted sideways and backwards at the same time, sort of leaning on each other, like a pile of landlocked driftwood. Trees all around had grown over and into it, with weeds and vines and scrubby palmettos sort of squeezing in.

Along the front ran an old fence, like the wall of a frontier fort. It was made of cedar stakes maybe ten foot high, but filled with gaps and buckling. The rest was enclosed by an old chain-link fence smothered by vines and rusted red in the few spaces you could see it. The parking lot out front had once been crushed oyster shells. Now it was thick with sandspurs and old cans. Nothing was left of the sign except two telephone poles crossed at the top and some scraggly letters still nailed to some boards. "CA T S TER   T RY" is all it said.

It wasn't much, but it would have to do. I pulled off onto the shoulder of the road and did a 180. When we edged up to the parking lot, I knew I'd have a job on my hands just keeping down the rebellion.

"Well, here we are. We'll be staying here for a couple of days, ladies." I was trying to jolly them up a little bit with the "ladies" and all.

"Where are we?" Vanessa asked. "What's this old dump?"

"It sure ain't Disney World," Chandra added.

"For real."

I nudged Heidi awake. It was time for some "moral support."

"Get up, Heidi," I urged, "this is that neat place where we're camping out."

"What camp out?" Heidi mumbled.

"I don't camp out. I get bites and swell. I get hay fever," Chandra announced. "My sinuses inflame."

"Oh, this place is approved by eight out of ten family

153

physicians. Just wait." I pulled the old Chevy around the side on what used to be a road. Now it was just two wheel ruts filling up with weeds.

"See, here's the secret entranceway." I stopped the car where the fence was clear of growth. The chain link had been jiggled loose from its post there and twisted up. The ground seemed soft—sort of squishy, even—and it was easy to squeeze underneath.

"No problem, come on in." Heidi snaked her way underneath on all fours, and Vanessa followed, just bending down and duck-walking right on through. Chandra was another story.

"I'm not coming in there," she said, pouting. "I'm not going anywheres 'cept Disney World, 'cause you promised me. And if we're not, you can take me on home."

"Pain-in-the-ass kid," Heidi growled under her breath. Vanessa waved for Chandra to come on in, but she just spun and stalked right back to the car.

"Never mind her, come on, let's look around." I took Heidi by the arm and Vanessa by the hand and escorted them around like we were sizing up a piece of choice real estate. The buildings were pretty much tumbledown, but the bank at least had a pretty good roof, and the door even closed if you lifted up and pushed toward the hinges. We went inside. It was dark except where cracks in the walls let in little slices of light. The shade felt good, being as it was late August. The dry cool wood smelled like old toast, a good smell, really. The boards cracked like they hadn't been walked on in years.

A long low counter with tellers' cages sat toward the back wall, and painted on the wall behind that was a faky-looking bank vault door, with shadows and everything to look all three-dimensional. I walked behind the counter and found that it was divided into three stalls, with low partitions between each one. Might be a good place to sleep. In the last stall my foot landed on something round and I almost crashed into the wall. I picked it up—a wine bottle half filled with cigarette butts. Guess we weren't the only ones to find our way to Cactus Territory.

"Jeez, it's spooky in here." Vanessa shuddered. I accused her of watching too many Scooby Doo cartoons.

"Great place to party, if you ask me." Heidi poked her head back out the door. "Man, you could get away with murder here. No neighbors, no police, no old lady to hassle you all the time." Old Heidi always had the wheels turning.

We went outside and walked around behind the buildings. Nothing much back there but some rusted old metal drums, a cracked toilet and a lawnmower without wheels.

"All the comforts of home," Heidi said, plopping herself down on the mungy old toilet seat.

"Yeah, if you live in a junkyard." Vanessa was studying her reflection in the rainwater at the bottom of one of the metal drums. "By the way, Nelse," her voice echoed out of the hollow drum, "what *is* the deal anyway?"

"What deal?"

"You know, kidnapping us, when we could go home or see Gramma. Bringing us down here to Florida. I think it's all weird."

"It *is* kind of weird, Ness," I admitted. "You see, when you and Mom left for Georgia, I figured you'd probably be coming back once Mom got it all out of her system. Of course, Dad went berserk right away."

Berserk? What's berserk—like drunk?"

"You know, wacko. He just sort of ran wild for a couple

155

of days. Burned the bed, shaved himself bald-headed, tore up Jungle Fever until the police called. I had to go get him. The General became his guardian, like, for a while, and Dad had to work off all the trouble he'd done. Then the General set him up in wrestling after that."

"You mean more dumb old alligators?"

"No, people, guys, legitimate matches. He's on tour somewheres right now. That's how we got to Georgia, matter of fact."

"So you come to get me, but why?" Vanessa lifted her head out of the drum.

"Why'd we come get you? Well, because you're my sister and I love you." She wrinkled up her nose. "And because I wanted us to be together. Not just you and me, but Mom and Dad, too. See, a while after Dad went nuts I got a letter from Mom. Said how she was doing just fine at Aunt Ruthie's, and how I was gonna have to be a man, like, and care for Dad. And then she said something about a lawyer and some divorce. Well, that sounded kind of permanent to me. I guess I just wanted to do something before it got too late."

"And this is it?" Vanessa shrugged and held out her arms to indicate how pathetic Cactus Territory seemed right then.

"No, *you're* it, honey," Heidi broke in. She came up behind Vanessa and cupped her chin in both hands. "You're the bait and your mamma and your daddy are the big fish."

"I don't want to be no bait. Specially in this old place. It's creepy." She broke away from Heidi and headed toward the fence.

"Well, you are the bait," I called after her. "At least for a few more days. So get used to it. And if Mom doesn't bite, if we never get them back together, them and us back at Gate o' Palms, or wherever the hell anybody wants to

156

be, if we all just get flushed right down the toilet of life then bullshit. Just BULLSHIT, because it won't be for want of tryin'."

"All right, Gator Man, just mellow down." Heidi grabbed me by the belt as I started off after Vanessa. "Just let her alone. It's a lot for a little kid to digest. Don't go messin' over her mind." Heidi slid her arm around my waist and pulled me sideways toward her. Vanessa stood with her back to us, her head down, at the fence. She was crying, that silent kind of crying where you kind of shiver down the back. I guess I felt pretty rotten right then.

"Go talk to her," I told Heidi. "Tell her I'm sorry for shouting. We got to get comfortable and used to each other. We're gonna be here for a while."

"Maybe we need to set up housekeeping. I'm starved." We hadn't had much to eat except breakfast and a couple of oranges. I told Heidi to take some money and buy some groceries. We had passed a grocery store maybe four or five miles back down the highway. We agreed that canned stuff—spaghetti, chili, fruit juice and Vienna sausages— would keep best.

"And take the girls. Get them something nice," I suggested. "And you'd better get a can opener," I yelled.

"Will do, sir," Heidi saluted like a scared army private.

"And maybe some toilet paper. Better make it a family pack," I yelled. After all, we still had to stay civilized.

26

So for the next three days we survived on junk food and Hi-C. We ate Slim Jims and Spaghetti O's out of the can and Oreos and Pringles. Chandra and Vanessa each had a private stock of Little Debbie Snack Cakes, and after three days of gobbling those things all over Cactus Territory the place looked like it was strewn with deciduous cellophane leaves. We got along pretty well, eating and playing charades and dumb kid stuff like that. But it wasn't bad, more like day-care in the jungle, with afternoon storms that chased us inside for maybe an hour at a time. We all got the runs, but nothing too bad, except once when Chandra went out behind a tree she thought she saw a snake. I had to spend the rest of the afternoon scouring the undergrowth, with a two-by-four, ready to kill. Never got it, but Chandra spent the night in the old Chevrolet with the windows cracked just enough to breathe.

Vanessa was the best pioneer of all of us. She went right to work exploring the territory and made one important discovery. In the far back corner by the fence was this real green squishy place that seemed to keep oozing up through the weeds and old leaves rotting on the ground. We pulled the weeds and leaves and junk away from there, scooped out the soft sand a little bit, and sure enough, we had our own little freshwater spring. I didn't let anyone drink out of it, and it was kind of murky brown. But it was the closest thing we had to running water, and it felt good on those sweaty days to go splash a little of that water on your face or under your arms or whatever. Still, we were beginning to smell a little rank—at least me and Heidi. I don't think Vanessa and Chandra were old enough for body odor yet.

On the third night the girls bedded down early, while Heidi and I sat outside just listening to the night. Every once in a while a car throbbed on by. Heidi lit a cigarette and watched it burn. It was a still night and the smoke rose straight up into the trees like fine threads.

"You're taking me into town tomorrow, into Lakeland," I told her. "It's time to start things moving."

"What's the plan? You asking for money?"

"Yeah. Just to keep up appearances. I'll call Ruthie's and set up a meeting. Where shall we say is the drop? I guess it doesn't really matter if we're planning on getting caught."

"What about right here? It's sure convenient."

"That's one idea, but it's not very glamorous. I was thinking of someplace like an airport, or the Statue of Liberty."

"That's in New York, fool."

"I meant someplace *like* that. A famous public place, with lots of people ogling around. The newspapers and TV guys love that stuff. They always do it like that in the movies. Plus, they don't like to shoot when there's so many people around."

"Shoot what?"

"The kidnappers. See, they can't risk hurting innocent people."

"Nobody's shooting me. That's not part of the deal, let's get that straight right now."

"In the movies, Heidi. I'm talking about the movies. No one's gonna shoot at us. Come on, let's go in, catch some sleep." I stood up and stretched. Heidi flicked her cigarette into the night and lit another.

"Go on, Nelson, I'll be right in."

I went into the dark, cool bank and felt my way along the counter. I found my stall, running my foot quickly over the floorboards to make sure no lizards or roaches had beat me to it. Slipping off my jeans, I emptied the pockets, removed the belt and rolled the pants into a pillow. I flopped on the floor and flattened out on my back. Two stalls away the girls were gurgling and snoring. Chandra was a child prodigy of snoring; probably her sinuses were inflamed.

I had just curled over into my modified fetal position number three when Heidi shuffled into her middle stall. After a snap and a zip her shorts fell to the floor. She let out a kind of muffled groan and half collapsed to the floor with a thunk. For the next half hour I listened to her turning on the hard floor, banging against the sides of her stall. Finally she got up. Bathroom, I thought, but then she was in my stall, lying right beside me.

"Put your arms around me if you're awake," she whispered, and I did.

"Nelson?" she said. I squeezed a little to let her know I

160

was there. Something was bothering her. "I hope this goes okay for you, with your family and all."

"Me, too."

She was silent for a while. "When we're back in school, are you going to ignore me like everyone else does?" she asked finally.

"No," I told her, but then I remembered her in school last year with that crummy gang. "It's just the things you do sometimes. And those guys you hang out with."

"Losers, I know. Sometimes you gotta take what you can get, that's all."

"Yeah, like me," I teased.

She grabbed one of my hands like she was going to twist the fingers off at first. Then she just braided our fingers together into a tight knot.

"As long as we're on the subject, you can promise me one thing," I whispered.

"What's that?"

"Promise me you won't do any more of those 'Half Nelson' routines anymore."

"Promise," she breathed, then I felt her kiss out of nowhere, like that time after the movies, only this time she wasn't kidding around.

27

Heidi and the girls drove me into Lakeland the next day. We parked at a disabled meter and looked for a place to eat. They wanted to go cruise a mall, but I said no way, we'd be easy pickin's all four of us, just like on the Wanted posters. I pointed out a newsstand and made Heidi swear she'd pick me up there at five that afternoon.

We ducked into one of those all-day doughnut places to plan our strategy. A morning newspaper was sitting on the counter, so I tucked that under my arm, and we found a booth by the front window. Some babe with silver finger-nails shuffles over to our booth. "What'll it be for you kids today?" she asks. Heidi's transfixed by her nail job, and the girls are gibbering about Disney World again, so I order us some Bavarian creams and milk. While I study the paper's front page the waitress disappears and returns, rattling our order down in front of us.

I'm just two bites into my Bavarian Swiss Creme-Filled Delight when I decide to skim the paper. Turning to page two, I flash on this little item:

DEVELOPER SEARCHES FOR DAUGHTER

Millionaire mall developer Chester R. Cheesman cut short a European vacation after learning of his daughter's disappearance in Georgia. The girl, Chandra Elizabeth, was staying with family friends in a small north-central Georgia town when she was apparently abducted from a vacation Bible school.

Also reported missing was seven-year-old Vanessa Gato, a friend of the Cheesman girl.

The California-based developer indicated he was eager to cooperate with the police in the search effort, although he did not rule out meeting any reasonable demand for ransom.

Police in Georgia have not revealed if there has been any contact with the kidnappers so far. They refuse to confirm rumors that one of the kidnappers may be a brother to the Gato girl.

Reports vary on the numbers of the abductors. Some witnesses claim as many as four people are involved in the plot.

A police spokesman has labeled the kidnappers' motives "unclear." FBI operatives in the Southeast have also become involved in the investigation.

"Can't you read without moving your lips?" Heidi mocked.

"Not this I can't," I answered, shoving the paper into her lap. "Here, read this to the girls."

She did all right, and they sat quiet as story time, their eyes round with amazement. Heidi finished with a flourish and rustled the paper back right on top of my breakfast.

"So we're famous—that's wonderful, right, girls?" I said. They glowed obediently. "Only problem is, they got it all backwards. Vanessa, you're the real victim. Chandra, she's just a tagalong."

"Whattaya mean I'm a tagalong?" Chandra shot back, bristling. "I can be a victim, too."

"What I really mean is, we're lucky to have you along, Chandra. See, without you, we'd hardly have a desperate criminal activity going on here. Your old man's big time, with all that ransom business. So relax, you're a celebrity."

Chandra seemed reassured, and everyone went back to their doughnuts. Except me. Cheesman wasn't ruling out a "reasonable demand." But how much was reasonable? Numbers revolved in my head: $100,000 . . . $500,000 . . . $1,000,000 . . . a million dollars from a millionaire, why not? He's probably got tens of millions, hundreds of millions.

"You all right, honey?" It was Fingernails. I'd been sitting there hypnotized by that story, counting all the unmarked thousand-dollar bills.

"Sure, fine. We're fine, thanks," I answered, coming out of my daydream. I asked her to bring a check, and she left as Heidi followed with the girls for a visit to the ladies' room.

Left alone, I started to worry. After a few minutes of serious consideration, I was ready to go call the police and turn us all into the Lost and Found, Juvenile Division. If my motives were that "unclear," it was time to shine a little light on my criminal mind. Besides, after the night before, I was ready to just go back to Cactus Territory and retire

164

there with Heidi, a couple of burned-out old teenagers finding true happiness among the palmettos of an abandoned ghost town. And Vanessa and Chandra could toddle away home, and Cheesman could count his money and buy Park Place, and Mom could do nails, and the Gator Man could wrestle to his heart's content until his Everlast high tops wore out.

But that was taking the short view. If I had dug my own grave, well, then, I guess I would just have to sleep in it.

And now for the World of Sports. I put my brain on hold and turned to the sports pages. Were the Braves still in the first division, has McEnroe had another hissy-fit, will the NFL players have their annual strike, how many running backs snort coke? I check the box scores on last night's games, read about some unknown pitcher who has a perfect game spoiled by a bunt single in the bottom of the ninth, when lo and behold, the old eyeball drifts to the bottom of the page and gets zapped from the blue for the second time that morning.

THE LAKELAND CIVIC CENTER
In Cooperation with Sandman Promotions Presents
AN ALL-STAR WRESTLING CARD

Bruno Sartucci vs. The Horrible Hrothgar
Pretty Boy Vic Elan vs. Kolnicki, the Powerful Pole

TAG TEAM ACTION

The Black Tong Bros. vs. Mountain Billy Walls
& Jersey Jim Lillo

PLUS

Kyle Markley vs. Destroyer Moyer
Chief Osceola vs. Corporal Kong
The Gator Man vs. Sammy Ray Finn

Tues., August 27, 7:30 P.M.
Tickets: $5.00 in advance, $7.50 at the door

DON'T MISS IT!

No way would I miss it. The old Gator Man was still down there at the bottom of the card, meaning he would still be wrestling the opening match. At least he was hanging on. He'd been on tour a week and a half, and it was close on five, six days since me and Heidi took off, Pensacola, Macon, Mobile, Columbus, Savannah, a day off, then Jacksonville and now Lakeland. I hadn't paid much attention to the schedule when we'd left, but that all came rushing back. I remember standing in the General's Jungle Fever office and hearing him read it off like the stopovers on a southbound Trailways bus.

By the time Heidi and the girls got back I must have been grinning like Little Miss Sunbeam—at least that's what must have first bothered Heidi.

"What's so funny?" she asked. "Are my shorts on backwards or what?"

"Or what," I said. "Read this." I handed her the paper, and she read as she slowly slid beside me into the booth once again.

"No kidding," she murmured, "tomorrow night, right here. He sure don't miss a beat. Amazing."

"What's amazing?" asked Vanessa. Obligingly, Heidi filled the kids in on Dad's skyrocketing career in the ring, but still Vanessa looked puzzled.

"But why's he wrestling?" She turned to me, accusingly. "Nelson, you said he'd be worried sick. You said he'd be looking for us, coming after us and all. And he's not doing any of those things, just wrestling. Dumb old wrestling."

"But he's got to," I answered weakly, realizing for the first time some small soft nibbles of disappointment down inside. After all, she was right. How could he just carry right along, business as usual, when his nearest and dearest

166

were missing in action almost a week? All's I could figure was the General must be keeping him locked in the van. Least it felt better to believe that.

"So can we go tomorrow night? Will you take us to see your father wrestling?" Chandra asked, tugging the paper from Heidi's hands. And then—rather sweetly, I gotta admit—she added, "I bet he looks just like you, does he, Nelson?"

"Sure—we can go, that is. As for looking like me, that's up to you to decide." Yes, I thought, the perfect setup—a rendezvous at ringside. Budding kidnapper reunited with loved ones. Family night at the Lakeland Civic Center. Time to get the wheels rolling, assemble the cast. . . . Mom would be there if I could just get word to her somehow. Once I had it figured, I laid it out for everyone right then and there, piece by piece, pausing only when Fingernails returned with the check.

But no one was buying, not just yet.

"I say it smells," Heidi announced, suddenly sulky. "And besides, how's it all gonna fit together, Mr. Mastermind?"

"Easy," I said, even if it wasn't. "I call back to Crosswell, tip off Mom or Ruthie, tell 'em where to make the drop, get the kids. Hell, the place'll be swarming tomorrow night."

"But what about Disney World? Don't forget you promised us Disney World, Nelson," Vanessa added.

"Besides, what's the hurry?" asked Chandra. "I was just gettin' to like this kidnap stuff."

"Yeah, you promised the kids, and besides, what about me?" There was a brittle edge to Heidi's voice now, something desperate I hadn't heard since that day at Lake Marjorie. "Good for you, good for the Gatos, not so good for Heidi T. It's all your little family picnic, always has been

167

from the start, but I was convenient, wasn't I, so now what? Wise up and butt out, that's the message—I can hear you loud and clear."

"But it's not like that. I'm not going to throw you to the wolves, for godssake. You're too important . . . to me, to all of us," but it wasn't convincing. I couldn't say it right, not there, not with the girls, not against the flat dark surface of Heidi's mood. So I tried something different. "What about your mom? Remember, this was for her, too, this was to pull her back, too."

"Crap, Nelson, that was crap from the start, and you could never tell could you? You're such a boy sometimes." Opposite us, Chandra and Vanessa shrank away from the harsh voice, stealing only broken glances at this sad and different Heidi beside me on the bench. "See, last time, when I took off I stayed with my grandfather. Then he died so I had to go back. This time around . . . well, hell, she'd arrest me for trespassing. I bet she's got 'Good Riddance' embroidered on her guest towels, and changed all the locks."

No use. She had left no space to maneuver, nothing to say. The girls were silent. I threw my arm around her shoulder and we sat. She shivered, once, under the weight of my arm but didn't push me away. Still, I could offer her nothing but talk.

"It'll be alright," I said. "Take it easy, we still need your help, we're still counting on you." Then, conspiratorially, I started spinning out the plan once more, pushing our attention back to now, blotting out the possibility of what might come after tomorrow.

"So you take the girls, get back to Cactus Territory right away. I'll stay here, contact Georgia, set things up for to-morrow night. Gotta scope the town out, figure where this Civic Center is. Leave it all to me. Deal?"

"Sure, deal, I suppose." The anger seemed gone, but now the voice was a vacuum, empty. "But after tomorrow . . . well, I've got options, don't think I haven't got options."

"Sure, we'll all have options after tomorrow," I said. What did she mean? I didn't ask. Instead, I got bossy. "Vanessa, you and Chandra go get in the car. And no more about Disney World for now. Let's get through this first, then we'll go anywhere you want. Now get." I shooed them out of the booth with the crumpled carcass of the paper, and they went skittering out the door like baby roaches under duress.

"You'll feel better tonight, once things are all set," I whispered to Heidi, giving her shoulder a squeeze. "Promise you'll come get me, say fiveish, at that newsstand back there on the corner. Just cruise by. I'll be ready." She heard but made no effort to respond, then stood up and seemed to drift out the door as if pulled by some invisible cord. Once inside the Chevy, she disappeared, leaving only a rectangle of white glaring windshield filled by the blank stare of an August sun.

I paid off Fingernails and got about five dollars worth of change. The phone booth in the parking lot outside didn't have a door, so once inside, I turned my back to the street and plugged up one ear. The phone at Ruthie's rang forever, then finally a pinched voice came on on the other end.

"Hello, Ruthie's House of Beauty."

"Mrs. Gato, please," I growled through a napkin over the mouthpiece.

"Not in. Can I leave a message?" Typical. But where could Mom be, I wondered.

"Yeah, write this down. . . ."

"Please hold while I get my notepad." Her notepad was in Hong Kong, judging from the time it took, or were they tracing the call? The operator broke in, "Your three minutes are up." I deposited the last of my quarters. The operator said "three more minutes, thank you," and finally Ruthie had her notepad. "Go ahead with your message now please."

"The Lakeland Civic Center in Florida tomorrow night at eight o'clock. Fill a shopping bag with tens and twenties." A nice touch, I thought. "The girls'll be there. No police or it's off." And I hung up.

I should have said something for Cheesman, too, but let him worry, I figured. And of course there'd be police all over, but that was the point.

I'll admit that right then I thought I had things pretty much under control. I was coming up aces in every hand. The boy genius was now an archcriminal ready to go into retirement with a happy family—his own—reunited. The girls were all nestled snug in their hideout, I thought, and later on we'd be together for one final night. It was all sort of like Wilderness Family, those drive-in movies Vanessa just couldn't get enough of, where everybody starves and freezes and fights bears and kind of overdoses on togetherness. And as for Miss Heidi Tedesco, well, she was part of it, too, a special secret part of the way I was feeling right then.

But man, did I stink. Five days in the same T-shirt and it had become a second skin. I started down the sidewalk looking for a cheapo-cheapo clothing store among all the old lady sundress boutiques. I had to go halfway out of town until I hit Dirty Dave's Army-Navy Outlet. They were having a back-to-school sale. I popped in expecting to get hit with a display of pencil boxes and Smurf raincoats, but it was just basic old army-navy trash: olive-drab ponchos,

170

all-weather combat boots, vinyl dress shoes and camouflage fatigues.

"Help you, Buck?" this clerk says. He's got a cigar butt between his teeth that could have been carbon-dated.

"Just looking," I said. I picked out a navy blue in a large and handed the guy a five-spot.

"Will that be all, sport?" I swear I had had this conversation before.

Back on the street, I peel off my shirt, throw it in a dumpster without waiting for the roaches to evacuate, then stretch into my navy blue. Feels real good, so good that I stroll right into a Big Boy and order up a combo deluxe and a piece of strawberry pie. Fat City, but it was my own little victory party. Later that afternoon I caught a movie (don't ask what it was, 'cause I passed right out and didn't wake up until halfway through the second show). By then the lobby clock said four, so I started back to the newsstand feeling maybe a little guilty. Poor old Heidi and the kids sweltering away the day while I napped in air-conditioned comfort with a belly full of strawberry pie.

28

Back at the newsstand I start eyeballing the skin mags, and this old potato-faced guy asks me how old I am. Then I start thumbing through a *Rolling Stone* and he asks me if I think he's running a library. So I take the hint and buy the *Rolling Stone*. I read about some band from Texas that eats raw armadillo before each concert, and by then it's five-thirty. No Heidi, no girls. So I read about some Japanese reggae band and a couple of record reviews and it gets to be almost seven.

I bought a *Popular Mechanics* with some article about how to convert your standard home bathtub into a whirlpool in two easy weekends, and a lot of junk about home computers and solar heating. But it was nine and still no Heidi. So I decided to give them until I got through a *Mad* cover to cover, and then I'd panic. By ten I was done with that. My eyes were shot from reading under the street lamp, the old potato face was ready to call the cops, and I was too fritzed to care.

All I knew was I'd made a mistake leaving Heidi in charge of the girls. She was the ultimate screwup, no matter what. I could think of a dozen monumentally stupid things she could have done, but it didn't do any good guessing. Whatever it was, I was pretty sure it would put the old jinx on our little escapade. Like what good is a kidnapper who misplaces the kids? All I could do was just hope they were safe somewhere and still in one piece. There were always plenty of creeps around who would like nothing better than to stumble across three helpless girls—well, two helpless girls and Heidi.

Suddenly her outburst at the doughnut place that morning started to make sense. She could come close to loving me, as long as she felt equal. But for Heidi "equal" meant on your own, high and dry, with family scattered in every direction. A reunion, however flimsy and farfetched it might be, left her feeling used up and useless and ready to fight back.

Or was it sabotage? Take the girls and run, her own little kidnapping to undermine my scheme, the cheapest of tricks. She had learned my Theory of Drastic Solutions very well indeed. Too bad she was dumb enough to think it would work on me. No teenage desperado was going to foul up my guerrilla maneuvers. If I ever saw her again, she'd better have eyes in the back of her head. Unless, of course, I was wrong.

I started walking out of town. It was miles and miles to Cactus Territory, but I didn't have anything better to do. The roads were still baking underfoot after a day full of sun. I stayed in the sand along the shoulder and stuck out my thumb. No luck. What cars there were were heading mostly the other way, back into Lakeland. The few cars going my way just flashed on their brights and whizzed right on by. No one wanted to give a ride on a deserted two-lane black-top going nowhere special. Probably get assaulted and battered. Probably had a hatchet in my pants. Guess nobody trusts anybody after ten o'clock.

Soon there's no cars either way. The moon disappears somewhere and the stars are still smothered behind this leftover haze. No wind, no movement, not even the good gush and grit of a draft breeze from an occasional semi. And suddenly watermelon, getting stronger as I walk along, the smell of watermelon thick and soft and slightly sour underneath as it gets closer. Until I'm right in the middle of them. Husks of watermelons around my feet, and rinds crammed into these two litter barrels, and the faint hum of flies still drinking in the sweet pink juice.

I turned away from the road and saw the outline of a picnic table against the black woods. I flopped on a bench, took off my shoes and leaned back. Running my arm over the tabletop, I could feel only the cool smooth painted surface of the wood. No sticky goo, no watermelon seeds, no globs of petrified catsup. In another second I was belly-down on the table, my toes wiggling over the end. Then I heard these words rattling out of my mouth: "Take care of us, please take care. And watch over Vanessa and Chandra, wherever they are tonight." And then I added, "Heidi, too. Watch over Heidi, too." And I didn't say Lord or God or Jesus 'cause I'm not really much for all that first-name-basis stuff. Besides, they know who they are if they really are listening all the time.

Anyway, it was bizarre, coming as it did from someone who gave up on "Now I lay me down to sleep" when I was six. Not that I was being born again or anything like that,

174

don't get me wrong. I was just making sure I hit every angle. And then I passed dead out, which probably wasn't going to help much, but sometimes it's the only thing left to do.

Even before morning really came full blast I lay there stiff, watching the first pale light filling in around the outlines of cabbage palms and palmettos. The flies still buzzed, thick and black, over the rinds of melons, and every so often a car would whine by on the highway. I remembered Heidi and the girls, half dreaming them really, Heidi with her red bandanna, skipping on her coffee-brown legs across endless parking lots, Vanessa and Chandra like pink-blond mice, nesting amid orange peels and candy wrappers in the Chevy's backseat. Above me the sky filled with blue and a morning breeze rattled in the palms.

I peeled myself off the table and walked upwind of the trash barrels to hitch a ride. I musta looked somewhat more trustworthy in daylight, because it wasn't more than three cars passed before I was sitting in the cab of a new blue El Camino. Fellow was delivering condensers to a plant in Frostproof. His units rattled in the back. He pointed to a cooler at my feet. "Help yourself," he said. I grabbed a pimento cheese sandwich and wolfed it down, followed by two swallows of coffee from his thermos. So much for breakfast.

When he finally dropped me at Cactus Territory, I walked around to the side where we had kept Mom's Chevy parked in the undergrowth. It was gone. Only a small patch of black goo left any hint of where the car had been, bleeding oil into the coarse brown weeds. I pushed through the hole in the fence and found the stalls in the old bank, looking for any traces of Heidi and the girls. Only a few cellophane

175

wrappers and an empty orange-drink can remained. No food, no clothes, even the toilet paper was gone. I looked for a note but there was none. Clearly they had gone for good, and if they had wanted me to know where, it would have to be by telepathy. Cactus Territory was back to being a ghost town.

I decided right then and there that I was tired of coming up empty every time I turned around. I mean, it was hard enough being an antisocial product of a broken home and all that. But it was even harder trying to do something about it when nobody was willing to cooperate. There I was, aspiring desperado, stranded and abandoned by my fly-by-night partner in crime, while my two victims just up and left with her, and all I had to show for it was a pimento cheese heartburn and a new blue navy-surplus T-shirt. I found the stall that just two nights ago Heidi and I had shared. I sat, trying to recall just for a minute her voice, her touch, but I couldn't. Nothing was real—love, family, even Cactus Territory—all fake, illusion. So let it go—and I did. And tears too, I suppose, but even they ran dry, evaporated.

So anyway, I figured I had two choices. Either sit on down and wait for Heidi and Vanessa and Chandra to show up, or just head on back to Lakeland and take my lumps. After about an hour of sitting around watching dragonflies mating in midair, I figured that maybe the second choice would be a little more productive.

It took me two rides and an hour of serious walking to make it back. By the time I hit the city limits I was pretty used up. My shirt was sticking to me front and back, until I had to strip it off and wring it out. My feet felt like baked potatoes, my nose ached with road dust, and little squadrons of gnats had latched on to me and kept flying into my ears. I've had better days.

I'm ready to drop right there when salvation appears. Big old bus rolls right up, *whoosh* go the air brakes, *woosh* goes the door, and a little puff of cool air tumbles right down on top of me. Before I know it, I'm standing up there dropping dimes into the glass box beside the driver and we ride off, me slouched out across two foamy orange seats, ready to roll forever.

By midafternoon I'd ridden on every city bus in Lakeland. They were air-conditioned and mostly empty and a good place to think. We were coming down to the final crunch. A few more hours and the Civic Center would be heating up with "live wrestling action." That meant Dad, the Gator Man, in full battle regalia: leopardskin unistrap, blistering boots, sixty-watt head. Was he becoming too good at being that wrestling "thing"? Anyway, he had a match. When he saw me, would he even care? But I had an appointment, and I'd have to keep it. Would Mom be there? I was desperate to see her—and scared witless at the same time. What would happen if I showed up empty-handed and told her, "Oh, by the way, Vanessa has disappeared with Chandra and this strange girl I know. Sorry about that, but these things happen." She would kill me is what she would do, and then sign me up for some home for juvenile offenders and hustle back to Georgia. She would check out on me just like she checked out on Dad. "You're hopeless, Nelson, just like your father, and you'll never amount to anything." And she'd be right, of course, and there wouldn't be a soul on this planet could blame her after what we put her through.

29

The Lakeland Civic Center was a huge vacuum cleaner of a building, round and squat and plunked down in the middle of three acres of asphalt parking lot. After I got off the bus, I bought a ticket and then strolled around the parking lot to check things out. Cars scattered all across the mostly empty lot, gathering in bunches under the apricot glow of vapor lamps. I headed around to the back of the auditorium where the service entrances were marked by stenciled "No Admittance" signs. For sure, there was the good old Gator Man van, covered with road dust, but still a radiant metalflake jewel among the ordinary specimens of cardom.

I was approaching the van for a closer look when a rent-a-cop lunges out from behind a silver-blue Trans Am and flips me a nervous look.

I slid around the other side of the van to escape his glare and stood there figuring my next move. Suddenly I realize

I'm looking at something very familiar. Faded blue and gray and slightly ancient, like some old confused Civil War veteran. It was the bomb, Mom's old battered Chevy, in the flesh.

I crack the door to check it out, and something lunges at me from the backseat.

"Scare me to death, why don't you?" Heidi yowls, half-asleep.

"Somebody oughta. Where've you been, where are the girls?" I ask her, sliding into the front seat as the rent-a-cop circles behind the car.

"Well, you know how we kept promisin' them we'd take 'em to Disney World and all?" I nodded, seeing what was coming. "So after we dropped you off yesterday morning, we didn't feel like going back to that old Cactus dump, so I said let's go. It was great, too. Have you ever been on that Space Mountain thing?"

"Yeah, I feel like I'm on it right now. So where are the girls, anyway?"

"Oh, they're both inside somewheres waiting to see your daddy wrassle," Heidi said. "Bought 'em their tickets just five minutes ago."

"Why aren't you with them? Come on, let's go in and get this thing over with." I reached across the seat for her lumpy shoulder bag and picked it up. It weighed a ton. "Here," I said, offering it to her. "Let's go."

"No. Put that down. I can't."

"What do you mean 'can't'? You mean you're scared, is that it, and you're ready to bail out just when it comes down to the hard part? Look, I'll take the responsibility if it's the police you're worried about. See, like we're still minors, like we talked about. Is that it, or what?" Her face was expressionless. I couldn't reach her. Just then, of all times,

179

she decides to lock into her space cadet mode.

"Not that exactly, Nelson." She stares out the window, suddenly avoiding my look. "It's more like I have an appointment, see."

But I didn't see, and I told her so. Then, "Who with, this appointment?" I asked.

"Just a guy, some guy named Christopher Something. But you know him a little, kinda."

"I do?" I was up to my neck in weirdness. I thought she was delirious.

"Sure, remember the guy in the VW, the guy you called the cowboy? That's Christopher."

I was going to be sick. I felt the bottom drop out of my stomach. "But how . . . where . . . how did you . . ." but I couldn't put a question together, there was no sense to it.

"Don't be so gaga, Nelson, I swear." Suddenly she was in control and I was the basket case. "He promised us he'd catch up, don't you remember?" I did, but I didn't want to. "Even as far back as Macon, he had told me that if we got separated we should meet in a week at Disney World. Well, yesterday was a week. It was all so handy, what with the girls wantin' to go and all, don't you see?"

"You can't walk out on me now," I told her. "That's what went wrong in the first place, all these people walking out on each other all the time. Whaddayou think, people are Kleenex? What about me and the Gator Man, and Vanessa, and my mom? Don't we count for anything?"

"Yeah, maybe to each other, but not to me. I'm not your wife, not your sister. You'll all have each other again pretty soon, and I'll be back to nothing."

"What about all summer?" I shouted. "What about Lake

Marjorie, and your spaghetti sauce, and the bloodworms, and Pensacola and Macon? And Sheriff Perkins, your old soap opera buddy? And what about two nights ago, what was that?"

"That was nice, it was all nice, but it's over. I don't belong, see. Maybe with Christopher I'll belong."

"Oh, so I'm last week's script and the Heidi Tedesco Show is moving on to the Christopher Cowboy episode. Christopher's a crud, Heidi, can't you see that? Nobody belongs with a crud." She had buried her face in her hands. Maybe I'd reached her. But when she looked up I didn't see any tears—only anger and hatred, for me, for taking away her last chance.

"No, he's not, he is not," she said very calmly. "He's taking me to Key West. He has a place in Key West and he rents sailboats, and I'm going with him. After Miami. First he has a transaction in Miami."

I could imagine what his transaction in Miami was all about. Lots of people were having transactions in Miami these days, and most of them were good for ten to twenty.

Right then I was full up to bursting with nothing left to say. My head was filled with thunderclouds. They could aerate my body with ice picks, but I'd be damned if I was going to let Heidi just sleaze off with that dribble of slime.

"There's no transaction in Miami without this," I shouted, snagging her bag from off the front seat. I bolted out of the car and ran off to the Civic Center. Heidi got a slow start but was coming after me all the same. I sprinted the circumference of the building, came around to the entrance and jammed my ticket in the usher's hand without waiting for my stub. Back outside, Heidi was being pushed away from the door by two guards. Without her bag there was no money, and without her money there was no ticket. She would have to wait for the cowboy to show if she wanted whatever was in that gym bag. I knew that's what she had been waiting for in the first place. And I knew that when he finally turned up, I would be hearing from both of them.

30

Inside the auditorium I walked to the back bleachers, keeping to the wall. Security men were stationed every hundred feet. Troopers waited far down by the ring under the pale fluorescent light. Were they waiting for me, were they here to pounce on the bagman when it came time for the drop? Or was it a normal precaution, in case of a riot, a guard against the crazies taking over the ring?

I spiraled down around the bleachers, my eyes fixed on one row at a time, scanning the seats in the opposite side of the stadium. They were filling from the bottom up, so my pace slowed as I neared the floor.

It should have been easy picking out Vanessa and Chandra in this wrestling crowd. If Heidi had deposited them in there she had done a good job of disguising them. Or maybe they were in the bathroom. Girls were always in the bathroom, especially when they traveled in pairs. Or, another thought, maybe they were in custody already, eating chicken noodle soup in a police van somewhere, under the watchful gaze of the keepers of the peace.

Still no trace of Mom, either. Would she show, had she gotten the message from Ruthie? Or had something better come up? I had forgotten to check the evening paper. Probably, I was pitching a shutout, and I was back to square zero. I had gone through Chandra, Vanessa and Heidi and now probably Mom had joined the ranks of missing persons. It would be just me and Dad. Half Nelson and the Gator Man.

I found a chair in the fourth row, at the far corner of the ring. The lights dimmed, voices hummed, and there was a smattering of applause. I kept my eyes zoomed to the entrance. People were still pouring in. Problem was, they were all in silhouette, outlined by the brighter lights of the lobby. Whatever happened from then on, I was flying blind, feeling my way to daylight from the bottom of a mine shaft ten miles down.

Then music—hard, fast rock stuff—started bouncing off the walls in louder and louder echoes. The chairs trembled with the bass notes. The audience clapped along, half with the music, half with impatience. Orange spotlights flashed on—it reminded me of some prison breaks, whatever that tells you about my frame of mind.

Then a voice came over the music. "Welcome to the Lakeland Civic Center and an evening of championship wrestling. But first, ladies and gentlemen, from our own Lakeland Junior College, the precision dancing of the Lakeland Wranglerettes." And then from nowhere these twenty highly developed girls in orange sparkled majorette outfits pranced into the ring wearing white Stetsons with chin straps. They shook and grinned and kicked and waggled their parts in exact time to the beat. But the audience wasn't having any of it. They were here for wrestling and they were angry. Buck-naked and passing out ten-dollar bills, the Wranglerettes mighta stood a chance. But the mood got ugly, and the Wranglerettes got off.

A lull followed as some maintenance man ran a push broom over the canvas ring. When he finished he got a huge ovation, and finally the announcer wove his way through the ropes and into the center ring. My gut lurched sideways; butterflies had invaded my abdominal cavity. The announcer gestured with his hand and a mike dropped out from the dark and bounced off his head.

"Welcome to the Lakeland Civic Center, home of outstanding attractions for the good people of Central Florida," he read from a card. "Tonight we present for your entertainment one of the finest wrestling programs to grace our fine facility. We'll be getting to our first event in just a few minutes, but first let me tell you about a special opportunity we have for you this evening, an opportunity to show the kind of compassion we have for some special children, even while you are enjoying the performances of these able-bodied giants in the ring. Tonight, between events, our staff will be coming to you with specially marked containers to accept your contributions for Jerry's Kids. Yes, in just a few more days, the annual Labor Day Telethon will once again—" But the crowd revved up into a chorus of boos, drowning out the little man and his speech.

Security guards glide down the aisles into the circle of light around the ring and the boos fade. The announcer plods on. As his droning voice continues, I see two figures coming row by row down the aisle opposite me across the ring. In silhouette the girl cranes her neck at each row, scanning the seats. The other silhouette is a blade-thin man wearing an oversized Stetson. He stands behind Heidi, searching the entire auditorium. Slowly, deliberately, they approach floor level and start around the ring to where I'm slouching down into my seat.

At my feet sits Heidi's bag—the contraband, the bait. I reach my hand deep to its bottom and feel for the gym bag . . . there! I grab its plastic handles and pull straight up, while potato chips, makeup, earrings and bracelets erupt in a drugstore lava on the floor. Finally the gym bag is free.

Still holding the bag by its handles, I stand and whirl it in great loops over my head. I watch Heidi and the cowboy as simultaneously they lock on target, like two retrievers posing after ducks. Suddenly they break for my seat, and just as suddenly I release the bag. It sails over their heads, rising in an arc that clears the ropes and lands center ring, where it slides right up to the announcer and comes to rest at his toes. He breaks in midsentence and drops his head. His jaw slackens, bewildered.

Heidi and the cowboy freeze, confused about their next move. Then Heidi sprints for the ring and does a belly whopper onto the canvas under the bottom rope. The cowboy, still frozen in his tracks, lifts his right arm, points his index finger at my forehead, cocks his thumb, and unloads a round of .38 caliber ill will right into my frontal lobe. It means he'll get me for this, I suppose, but right then I was more concerned about Heidi.

After unloading his threat, the cowboy strolled real casual up to the ring, slowly parting the ropes, giving it the old nonchalant. Heidi, meanwhile, had scrabbled right across the ring and was lying curled up on her side, tucking the gym bag into her folded body. The announcer had retreated to a neutral corner, like the first event had already started unannounced. The cowboy stood against the ropes, gesturing at Heidi to come along.

And that's when the police descended upon them. It was bizarre, a ringside pantomime of cops and robbers, and the whole audience sat spellbound like they were watching some sunrise service at the Vatican. A pair of cops lifted Heidi, still with the gym bag lodged into her gut, and carried her out of the ring. A plainclothesman sidled up to the cowboy, cuffed him like the whole thing had been rehearsed a hundred times, and escorted him up the aisle behind Heidi.

Suddenly the whole audience exploded into a thundering ovation: a definite law-and-order crowd. By the time they hit the top steps Heidi and the cowboy were celebrities, walking a gauntlet of popping flashbulbs. Seemed like everyone had a little piece of the sun.

I watched as Heidi disappeared into the bright light of the lobby, then I stooped to scrape her possessions off the floor and replace them in her shoulder bag. She might need them soon enough, and maybe there'd be a chance I could see her, explain why I had to do it. Like if it was between turning her in and just losing her altogether I would take the lesser of the two rottens.

31

As I sat back in my chair again, it seemed to float through the floor like in those childhood dreams where the bed floats you up into sleep. I had definitely checked out on reality and was merging with the cosmos. "Take hold," I heard myself saying, and I grabbed the hard metal edge of the chair. "Now focus," a voice said, and I stared into the ring as the announcer regained the microphone. I had to take control now; it was time to hold on for one last shot.

"And now for our first match of the evening. A young man from Turlington, Missouri, and the first time ever in a Florida appearance, at 287 pounds, Handsome Sammy Ray Finn." Over the ropes with a side-straddle hop soars Handsome Sammy Ray. He stands dead still in ring center and slowly uncoils the belt to his robe. The robe slithers down arms bursting with muscle and reveals a body that could have been chiseled out of marble by Michelangelo. Sammy flexes into a pose for each of the four sides of the ring, his body rippling to attention in a bundle of lumps and bulges. Whistles and hoots of appreciation greet each new pose until finally Sammy lifts his glorious Hollywood profile and blows kisses to the howling mob.

"And from down Palmetto way, here in the great state of Florida, half human and half reptile and one hundred percent pure meanness, at 270 pounds, say hello to the inimitable Gator Mannnn. . . ."

Then into the ring scrambles not the Gator Man, but the General, pulling himself crablike up the side and through the ropes. Dressed in pith helmet and white dinner jacket, he salutes the audience with his knob-top walking stick. They respond with catcalls and peals of laughter. The General is satisfied. He walks to ringside and pries the ropes apart with his stick. Then, through the gap, lopes the Gator Man in his green satin robe. He laps the ring, staring into the darkened audience with sad, searching eyes. Sammy Ray and the General get tangled in an argument, but the Gator Man just settles into his corner and removes his robe. His head glistens pale green in the white light, his sloping body heavy and soft next to the sculpted frame of Sammy Ray.

"This event is the best two out of three falls, no time limit," the announcer intones. "Your referee tonight is Artie Lopez." Artie pops into the ring as the announcer slithers down through the ropes. He is bald and mustachioed, and wears his pants hiked up halfway to his armpits. He grabs the mike as the two wrestlers face off in center ring.

"Gentlemen, you know the rules. No punching, no biting or gouging, no hairpulling. You get two warnings and then it's a forfeit. If I direct you to your corner, you're going to

189

stay there until I tell you to wrestle. Now let's have a good clean match when the bell rings."

In the corner above me Sammy Ray fusses with his hair, primping like a schoolgirl. The Gator Man holds on to the ropes and lowers himself into a few final deep squats. At the bell, Sammy Ray launches himself into midair, touches down in center ring and goes roaring around the ropes. Dad just strolls out and stands watching. He refuses to chase. Sammy goes slingshotting off the ropes, from side to side and back again. He is a blur, showing off his speed and strength until the Gator Man seems to fall into a trance. Sammy leaps and vaults like a mad kangaroo, circling closer and closer. Dad crouches, waiting for the attack. Already he is drenched in sweat, a small dark triangle staining the seat of his trunks.

The display continued. Dad's crouch wilted. His adrenaline seemed to drain and evaporate right into the darkened arena. His eyes had stopped following Sammy Ray's gyrations, instead glazing over with fatigue.

That's when Sammy Ray caught him the first shot. Instead of feinting and dodging around, he lit into midair and caught the Gator Man with a wicked flying dropkick to the head. Dad melted to the floor. He heaved for breath like a beached whale, his chest rising and falling. Slowly he worked his way to his knees and *blam* another flying dropkick flattened him to the canvas. Then the third time, up and *blam*.

I waited for the Gator Man to rally. It should have gone like that. He rose again and headed to the ropes, half falling against the turnbuckles. His right foot pushed down the bottom rope; he was trying to get out. The General jabbed the walking stick against his breastbone and nudged him off the ropes and back into the ring.

190

The next minutes slowed to centuries. Sammy Ray tormented Dad, punishing him for no good reason, dragging out the match second after agonizing second. Instead of simply pinning the Gator Man, he attacked and retreated, attacked and retreated. A body slam, and the Gator Man would rattle off the canvas and crawl to ringside. Sammy Ray would latch on to his cracked old Everlast boots and drag him back for more punishment—helicopter, backbreaker, paralyzer, knee drops—keeping just this side of extermination. The referee said nothing and the slaughter continued.

The problem was, everybody was probably figuring it was the old possum routine. But I knew better. I knew my dad well enough, and I knew he had a lot of heart. He could take punishment, absorb practically anything, and still have something left. No matter how bad it got, he could always come back, one way or another. But not tonight, something was missing, his eyes had said as much before the match even began. He had shown up for the match, but he left his heart behind. Even the great rage and fury, his double nemesis, had deserted him.

Another thundering body slam left the Gator Man flattened in a corner. His shaven pate had deepened from pink to crimson. His body twitched once, and he curled over onto his side, arms tucked against his chest, legs pulled up toward his head. He was not getting up this time.

That was enough. *"Stop it, stop it, leave him be, he's my father!"* I flew up the aisle. Security men grabbed for my feet and got air as I rolled into the ring. I took my father by the ankles and spun him onto his back. His eyes were closed. The referee grabbed at my leg. "Get out of here kid, you're in trouble already." I planted a foot in his gut and shoved him across the ring. Turning back to my father,

I cleared my mouth and pumped a first breath into his lungs. It was all I could think to do.

I pulled away to fill my lungs. A shadow came across my dad and me, eclipsing the bright lights from above. It was Sammy Ray. I didn't know whether he was there to help or just coming back for more. It didn't matter. I threw my whole weight against him, thrashing and kicking blindly. He lifted me to eyeball level and tried to speak, but I sunk a hand into his Adam's apple and dug my fingers in as deep as they would go. Gasping for air, he dropped me and tripped and we both crashed downward onto my father's chest. I landed a split second earlier, and when Sammy Ray slammed on top, smashing me against my dad, I heard the faintest click and snap, like a lock rattling shut at the end of a long, empty corridor.

"Dad, Daddy, come on, don't give up," I pleaded into my father's face. "It's me, Dad. Nelson, it's your old Half Nelson, come on." But he just lay there, limp and still. I felt the weight lift off me and saw Sammy Ray taking my father's pulse. He was joined by the referee, who had finally caught on that this was no act.

"Will Dr. Herbert Fine please report to the ring at once. Dr. Herbert Fine, please report at once." The announcer's voice boomed into the now-silent auditorium. "And will the guards please remove this young man from the ring?"

Not yet, buddy, not quite yet, I thought. Scrambling to my feet, I pushed the announcer aside and grabbed the microphone. "Mrs. John Anthony Gato, if you're out there, please come down. Are you there, Mom? Daddy's hurtin' and we need you."

Instantly, hands were clamping down all over me. I broke loose long enough to land a solid shot on the jaw of a state trooper. Then I was pinned to the floor, spreadeagled, with each arm and leg squeezed by about three hands each.

"Stay put, buster, and you'll be just fine," a voice came at me from above the spotlight.

"Get the cuffs, get 'em on 'im."

"Let's get 'im outta the ring first. Ain't no public show."

"Whatever, just hold on. This could be the kid."

I felt myself being lifted and passed out of the ring. I craned my neck to check on Dad. He was leaving the ring, too, strapped on a stretcher, still unconscious.

Then in the middle of all these rough male voices came the sweetest little urchin voice I've ever heard. "Put him down, please. He's my brother and he isn't very dangerous, so put him down."

Vanessa!

Miraculously, they did put me down. I stood now below the ring, looking for the source of that sweet voice. Vanessa slid between two officers, and I swept her up in a hug.

"Ness, Ness, thank God."

"Nelson, you're choking me," she gasped out. She turned to the nearest uniform. "See, he is so my brother. And that Gator Man is our daddy, too. Se let my brother go."

"Not quite yet, sweetie," he said.

"Vanessa, you're terrific," I said, finally setting her back down. "Where's Chandra? Is she all right?"

" 'Course she is, her daddy came and got her—at Disney World. Did you hear we went to Disney World?" I said I'd heard.

"Ness, is Mom around? Are you here with Mom?"

"It's Mom, see?" she said bobbing her head toward the seats. In the murky light I could barely see Mom, in discussion with a man in a business suit.

"That's Lieutenant Jamison. They're discussing what to do with you," Vanessa told me.

Jamison nodded to the troopers surrounding me. He led Mom and Vanessa down the aisle and out a back entrance, with the troopers hustling me along behind. They put us in the back of an emergency vehicle—me still in handcuffs—and locked the door. Dad was in there already. An attendant sat by his head, reading gauges and holding an oxygen mask to Dad's face. We roared off for the hospital with Jamison and two troopers following five feet behind, and another car in front leading us through the parting traffic ahead.

The Gato family was together once again! Nelson the Magnificent had done the impossible. Still, it was some reunion. Me in handcuffs, with a promising future in extortion, Dad rigid on a stretcher and living off borrowed air, Vanessa at seven going on forty with the home life of a gypsy, and Mom, huddled in the corner, with her empty eyes burning a hole in the wall over my head. We got to the hospital in ten minutes. Not once did Mom blink or speak or so much as shuffle her feet. I wasn't even sure she knew I was there.

32

"It'll be a couple of hours before the doctors have any news for you. Make yourselves comfortable. There's coffee and soft drinks in the machines, magazines here. If you have any questions, please ask the nurse at the desk." And so we were welcomed to the waiting room by this very nice Japanese-looking nurse.

After we all sat down, Mom turned to Lieutenant Jamison. "Can't you at least take the cuffs off him? He'll be all right."

"Of course we can." He produced a key and clicked my hands free. "There, that's much better, isn't it, son? You just relax here, and after we hear from your father's doctors we can take it from there. You'll have to be booked. A hearing will be scheduled as soon as possible. It'll save you from having to change schools if that's necessary." He patted me on the shoulder, trying to be real paternal and comforting.

"Change schools?" Mom broke in. "What's going to happen to him? Will he go to jail?"

"Oh, a lot depends on the hearing. Your son has accumulated a backlog of some pretty serious charges—kidnapping, attempted extortion, operating a vehicle without a license, uh . . ." He sat in a molded chair beside me and started picking lint off his socks. "And tonight, of course, there was resisting arrest and assault, with that incident in the ring."

"What does all that add up to, Lieutenant?" Mom asked.

"Well, of course, he's a minor, but these are serious charges. Cheesman wants blood—*wanted* blood, I should say. He's pleased that his girl is in such good shape. And she had a ball. Still, he says he'd like to speak to the boy, your Nelson, he means, before going ahead with anything. Remember, kidnapping is a federal offense—there is no such category as 'unintentional abduction.' We're not exactly talking misdemeanors, understand. And then, again, a lot depends on the, uh, family situation."

Mom dropped her head when she heard the bit about the "family situation." "Our family situation . . . well, it's unsettled right now, as you know—"

"It doesn't have to be, Mom," I broke in. "Settle it, just go on and settle it. Come back to Palmetto and let's just get back to normal."

"Normal . . . just what is normal, Nelson? Is tonight normal, is your father in there trying to stay alive normal? Is what happened to Vanessa normal?"

"Sure it's normal, for us it's normal. Dad was only trying for his old dream and he finally got the chance. And me, why do you think I did all this dumb junk? I wanted you back, that's why, I wanted us all back."

"I will not be pressured, Nelson. Not into coming back,

196

not into anything. You can't twist a person's arm to make them change. A family needs something more than dreams."

Everyone in the waiting room was looking at us. Jamison sort of stared them back to their own business. He coughed into his fist and broke in with this very calm, soft voice.

"You see, Mrs. Gato, that's where Nelson is somewhat fortunate. He does have a mother and a father, regardless of how unstable your relationship is. That Tedesco girl, we can't even locate her parents, much less—"

"Heidi? You got Heidi? Where is she, is she all right?" I pictured her in jail. Sad. But safe.

"Yes, we have Miss Tedesco. And a friend. Maybe you could tell us everything you know about Mr. Buscaglia, how you got involved with him."

"Buscaglia? You mean the skinny guy with the hat?" Jamison nodded. I took him back through the whole story, from Macon, to the roadside at Eulee Springs, right down to that very night at the auditorium.

"Yes," he agreed, "and your sister and Miss Cheesman have described the meeting at Disney World. Now, if you could just tell us what you know about the contents of the bag, we'd be interested to hear."

"The bag. Oh, that." Mom had suddenly tuned in to our interview, tugging nervously at her lower lip. "Well," I continued, "I suppose it's the usual, cocaine or heroin or whatever they're selling these days. I mean, I didn't open it up or anything. I just assumed—"

Jamison broke into a little chuckle. "Well, close, pal, but on this one at least you and the girl are innocent as babes."

Mom smiled her polite little smile, relieved. I was stumped, though. "What was in the bag, Mr. Jamison?" I asked.

Jamison patted me on the knee. "Let's just leave it like

197

this, son. Ask yourself how much sense it would make for somebody to be taking illegal drugs *to* Miami—where everything comes *out* of. It's this hemisphere's discount drugstore. No, sir, folks shopping in Miami need money, cold hard cash, like that."

"Oh, so the bag was filled with money—I get it." But then, I didn't get it. "But what's illegal about that?"

"Nothing, unless it's funny money."

"Counterfeit?"

"Not exactly, son, just a little exotic. You might say Miss Tedesco's friend was prepared to pay the currency of a particular country to a particular agent of said hostile country for certain goods—but that's enough. All I can say, if you're gonna counterfeit this stuff, you better practice your Spanish. Your friend Heidi, too. Now let's drop it."

"Don't call that Heidi my son's friend, if you please, Lieutenant Jamison." Mom was ready to launch into Heidi.

"Aw, Mom, Heidi's no more to blame than anybody. She just *looks* tough. She helped me with all this. Heck, she's partly the reason you're here, she's been like a—"

But Mom wasn't having any.

"After the police tracked you this far, Nelson, they had to call Aunt Ruthie, and she said call Palmetto and Grams said call Lakeland, because I'd already told her I'd be over here for your harebrained scheme. And so they called every motel and hotel in Lakeland, and when they finally found me it was off to Disney World to collect Vanessa before they dragged me out here because I had to claim you or the police would lock you up right away like they did your little Heidi."

"Then you knew it was us—me—all along?" I felt some shrinking inside, like some dumb kid playing cops and robbers until his mother tells him to come wash his hands and

198

get ready for supper. Zoom, the incredible shrinking Nelson; Half Nelson lives.

"Oh, they caught on pretty fast. The Sunday school lady described you, and Mrs. Nadeau, who runs that little store outside Crosswell. And some sheriff in Eulee Springs reported you earlier, and that seemed to fit. And the car was gone—who'd want to steal that old thing? Nelson, it's hard to believe I raised you up from a baby, that you'd go and do something like that."

"Why didn't they stop us then, if everyone knew so much?"

"They thought they had you once or twice. I don't know; you just disappeared. I swear we thought we'd seen the last of you."

"Must of been when we camped out south of here, place called Cactus Territory," I said.

"Well, whatever it was, we got that call and knew you were on drugs or something. Really, a shopping bag full of tens and twenties! You must think people are plain stupid."

By then I was downright microscopic and looking for a hole to crawl through. "Is Chandra okay? She wasn't really part of the deal, you know; she sort of invited herself along."

"Yes, Chandra *and* your little sister are all right, no thanks to you. But you should have seen them, poor dears, when I went to their rescue at Disney World. Your beloved Heidi just up and left them right there, no money, nothing, without so much as a . . . well. Vanessa"—she darted a hand out, grabbing Ness by the wrist and reeling her in around right in front of us—"tell your brother what happened to you and Chandra, and how you're thankful to be alive."

"You mean about the Pirates, Mom?" Vanessa asked.

"Yes, the Pirates of the Caribbean. Tell Nelson how they found you. Go on."

Vanessa arranged herself like she was lead angel in the

school play, then began: "Okay, now after we got to the place, Chandra and me wanted to go to Fantasyland. So we all got tickets and the money was all used up and we took the monorail over and that's where we got off."

"Go on, dear," Mom coached.

"So Heidi says, 'Here are your tickets, have a good time, and I'll meet you outside the Haunted Mansion in an hour and a half.' So me and Chandra went on Dumbo and Peter Pan and these teacups and finally we went into the Pirates of the Caribbean. But Chandra said she would get a nervous stomach 'cause she was scared about dark places, and there was a lot of noise comin' out, so I said don't be chicken, so we got in a boat and when we got to this part where you go around a bend real fast a really gross guy with warts and knives jumps at you, and Chandra just absolutely got all freaky and jumped out of the boat even though they have these safety things that go over your lap like this to keep you in." Vanessa exhaled and got her breath for the big finish. "And so that's when I jumped in, too, 'cause Chandra is my best friend and everything, and you're s'posed to help your best friend when they get in trouble, so I did. And then those men pulled us out and took us to this place underground where the lost children go and they asked us stuff about our parents and stuff, and this nice lady started making phone calls all around, and we had lunch and got to meet Mickey Mouse and they gave us these two really neat Magic Kingdom lunch boxes for school, and that's when Mom showed up."

"And do you know what?" Mom broke in. And of course I didn't know what, but I had the feeling I was going to find out.

"Do you know Chandra's daddy flew from Paris, France, all the way down here after your little phone call to Ruthie's?

An important man like that. And if you could have heard what he had to say about all this, you'd just thank your lucky stars that Lieutenant Jamison has you in his custody right this very minute."

Mom seemed farther away than ever, farther away now than even Aunt Ruthie's in Georgia. I had done it all for her—well, maybe for myself, too—but for her mostly and for all of us. Now sitting just seats away, she had become some kind of other person, unknown, just a sad-eyed woman pushing into middle age, with a roomful of other strangers late at night in some hospital waiting room still as death.

"Come on, Ness, let's walk." I pulled Vanessa by the hand and we walked into the parking lot. Jamison followed us to the door but let us go on by ourselves. He knew I wouldn't bolt this time. We walked around the hospital. Vanessa stopped at every bench to stare at the windows. Some were still lit, some dark. In some we could see nurses floating like spirits, white creatures with no legs, drawing curtains and arranging bouquets. We invented a patient for each lighted window. For Vanessa they were all filled with mothers and fresh babies, or kids with tonsils or chicken pox. I kept mine to broken legs and nose jobs—no use bringing up cancer or leukemia or damaged hearts. She would have time to find out about that later. After we had imagined our way around the whole building, we got back to the waiting room entrance, where Jamison was still standing. Mom was not there.

"Your mom's gone to see your father. The nurse got her maybe ten minutes ago." He checked his watch. "Go ask at the desk, Nelson. He's in room 174."

33

I hurried Vanessa through the corridor so she wouldn't have too much time for sightseeing. Then I knocked weakly on the door to Dad's room, and Vanessa hid behind me as we entered. Dad was stretched out on his back in this massive aluminum bed. Tubes and hoses spiraled out of his nose, others went into his arms. Ropes and pulleys suspended from the ceiling bound his legs and cradled his lower torso. He could have passed for Gulliver in the land of the peewee doctors, lashed and hog-tied a hundred different ways.

"My son, the kidnapper. Who's that hiding behind you?" Dad watched us through lids drooping at half-mast. Mom sat sort of stroking the bed rail like it was my father's arm.

"What a couple of sorry wretches the cat drug in. Come on over here, give the old Gator a kiss." He tried a weak gesture with his arm, but it was too clogged with tubes to

202

move. A bag of blood hung above his bed, draining through a needle into his arm.

Vanessa couldn't reach his lips, so she planted one on his forearm where the needle penetrated his vein. I'm not much of a kissy type, but I gave him a manly smack on the tip of his bristly head.

"Are you gonna live or what?" Vanessa asked.

"Let's vote on it," Dad said.

"I vote yes," Vanessa said throwing up her arm. "Come on everybody, put your hands up for Daddy." I raised my hand and watched Mom's embarrassed smile. Vanessa held her arm stiff and upright, waiting for a unanimous vote. Slowly Mom released her grip on the bed's rail and flicked a limp hand through the air like she was swatting a fly.

"Hooray, Daddy's gonna live, it's a majority for Daddy."

"But it's gonna take more than happy thoughts and pixie dust, Vanessa," Mom said. "People don't just mend because you want them to."

"But it helps—and so does pixie dust if you've got any."

A bearded bear of a man came swirling into the room, both hands plunged into the pockets of his lab coat. One hand darted out and patted Vanessa on the head. "Hello, I'm Dr. Blythe, and you must be the Gatos. Mrs. Gato?" he asked, extending his hand. Mom rose, shook his hand, and sank to her chair again.

"I confess, Mr. Gato," he continued, "you're the first professional wrestler I've ever had the pleasure of treating. Must be a rough way to keep the kids in shoes if your condition is any indication." It was sort of a joke, but no one was in a laughing mood. He got down to business. "Well, the diagnosis is simple enough, folks, but the cure will take some time. Mr. Gato, you've got a bleeding ulcer.

Stress, nerves, diet, they could all be to blame. Anyway, that explains your blacking out. You lost a lot of blood tonight, and we're trying to get your level up. After that, maybe surgery, but that depends on the extent of your ulceration. Basically, your stomach has a hole in it, and it's bleeding. More tests should tell us how much."

We all tried to absorb that. Vanessa wilted into an empty chair, both arms clasped across her stomach, like she was sharing Dad's misery. Mom's hand dropped to the bed, covering Dad's hand as it fretted the sheet into a wrinkled ball.

"Of course, the traction is another problem altogether," Dr. Blythe continued, twanging one of the cords stretching from Dad's legs like it was a guitar string. "This particular device is to immobilize your legs and torso, Mr. Gato. It seems you must have had quite a lot of weight on your spine, maybe a bad fall. Either way, what you've got are some fractured vertebrae—second and third lumbar, to be precise. Take that and your other problem, and it looks like you've got some healing to do, some real slow healing. As far as the wrestling goes, I wouldn't even worry about that right now."

That's when I remembered the sound, the faraway sound of something cracking that I had heard earlier that evening. "I did it, Dad. I'm the one responsible for how your back got messed up so bad. I'm sorry, in case you want to blast me when you get better." He hadn't remembered a thing, and I didn't have to say anything about it. But I wanted to. I explained how I ran into the ring when he passed out, and how Sammy Ray and me came slamming down on top. I even told him about hearing that far-off crack. I felt rotten, telling it.

"No one's gonna blast you, son. I had it coming, you

204

could say." His voice was weak but there was no anger.

"You didn't have anything comin', you just—" I protested, but he broke in on me right there.

"Sure I did. Remember that old cow gator down at the General's place?" he said, meaning Jungle Fever. I nodded. "Well, you might say she caught up with me tonight. My spine for hers. The old mama gator came back tonight and took the old bull with her. That's all."

That was about all for that, I figured. Dad was beginning to believe in the vengeance of an old dead alligator's ghost.

"It all goes back to Heidi and her grape sno-cone if you ask me," Vanessa added.

"Let's drop it, Vanessa; your father needs his rest," Mom said.

The doctor agreed and excused himself. He would be back in the morning, he said. And then he left us alone for five more minutes.

"How is she anyway? Is she here tonight, that Heidi? She's a pretty nice kid, Nelson. She cared about you. I think she was a little soft for you, old boy." Dad gave me a little wink.

"She's right where she belongs," Mom said.

"Too bad," Dad said. She's got spirit at least, the old spit and grit. Glad to see you've got some, too, son. This kidnapping plot has a certain ring to it, a certain touch of the old Gator flair. This world needs a few good kids who aren't afraid to get a little mud on their shoes. It's a swamp, all swamp, and any kid who's not afraid to wade right into the muck is bound to get the jump on all the ordinaries out there, sucking down soda pop, with the old headphone disease."

"Johnny Gato!" Mom was furious, but for the first time the room didn't sound like a morgue. "And you call yourself a father. . . . Do you know this son of yours is in the custody of a policeman? Do you know there's a Lieutenant Jamison waiting out there in the waiting room this minute for Nelson to come out? Do you know he's going to have a record as long as your big overdeveloped arm? Johnny, *you are a disgrace.*"

Mom jumped up, snapped her purse under her arm, and started dragging Vanessa out of the room. "Come along, children, let's get out of here."

We followed along in Mom's wake as she plowed into the waiting room. There we picked up Lieutenant Jamison and saw another familiar face—General Lee was at the nurse's station, asking directions to my dad's room. In a flash, Mom detoured up behind him without him ever knowing it. And when he turned she caught him *blam* right upside the head with her purse.

"Stay away from my husband, just stay away. He's not your dummy, he's a man and my husband and you just stay away. Or I'll have this officer arrest you for harassment." She grabbed Lieutenant Jamison and pulled him smack up into the General's face and shook him a little like she was brandishing a baseball bat. The General retreated behind the nurse's desk. Mom pivoted and tore out of the hospital, still dragging Jamison by the sleeve.

By the time Jamison got us to a motel, Mom and Vanessa had pretty much passed out in the backseat. Jamison was humming "Columbia, Gem of the Ocean" as he carried first Mom, then Vanessa, and deposited them on the beds inside. He told me to get some shut-eye and be ready for the old legalistic meat grinder first thing in the morning. I said sure, and promised one more time that I would stay put. I was in my mom's custody, he reminded me, and I

206

told him sure again and then added, "That's the whole point of everything, in case you're looking for a motive." He gave me a look like I'd just cursed his ancestors in Sanskrit. "Save it for tomorrow," he said, sliding into his car and slamming the door. I stood on the porch and watched his car disappear into the night, leaving only two fine threads of trailing red light.

I sat on the porch. Out on the street the cars whizzed by, crossing and passing, their lights intersecting, then gone. Toyotas and Buicks, Fords and Hondas and Volkswagens, endlessly passing, coming and going here and everywhere, always out there somewhere, coming and going. That, I suddenly realized, was the very heart of it, this constant moving, this leaving and arriving, this infernal, eternal coming and going. Restlessness, that had been the disease that had finally done in my dad, eating him up from inside and pulling him along from the misery of his "ordinary" life to the irresistible lure of his Gator Man dreams. It had infected Mom, too, who wanted nothing more than to stay put, but who had to leave us until I pulled her back again. And Heidi, who seemed to live off the movement and the chaos and the noise, who seemed to thrive most when the next day was a complete unknown. And good old Vanessa, caught up in the middle, and me, trying to fix it all, to give everybody a center, some gravity to pull it all together into some semiharmonious orbit.

And that's when I looked up at the planets and the stars. Sure enough, they were still up there, trying their very best to shine their way through the thick night of Florida's hazy August sky. And all their reassuring patterns, the Orion and the dippers and Ursus the bear. They are all really streaking through space, I remember hearing once,

207

scattering across the emptiness of space at the speed of light. More movement, more leaving. Maybe that was how it always was.

And then it hit me, that out there in the night the minute hands on all the clocks of Florida pushed slowly, invisibly, past midnight. It was August 28, and by some miracle I had survived my first sixteen years on this planet. I just sat there and listened, thinking how we'd all have to start over again in the morning, my birthday morning and every morning, kick it all in gear one more time.

34

So we scrape along, back now at Gate o' Palms, keeping an uneasy truce in which Dad lives with Grams, and Mom and Vanessa pretty much have taken over the old family trailer. And me? I'm still the shuttle diplomat, or at least the original time-sharing son. As wise King Solomon once said, if you can't chop your kid in equal halves, at least live in adjacent trailers. One night I'll spend with Dad, wolfing corn curls and watching Championship Wrestling on the tube; one night I'll join the ladies for ice cream and Scrabble by candlelight. I run messages, bills, leftover casseroles back and forth between trailers. It's not the sort of arrangement I'd figured on when I got started with all my frontal assaults on the broken home. But at least if they ever change their minds, it's a short little walk to ask for forgiveness.

Dad says he's going to grow wings and fly off to Pizza Hut if he has to eat any more cottage cheese. But the doc says his stomach is healing and the therapy is getting his legs back in tune. The insurance money helps with bills— gotta give the General the credit for that, say what you want; he was watching out for my dad after all. Meanwhile, the funny one-strap suit, the cracked old Everlast high tops are back in the navy trunk, maybe for good. Dad hasn't mentioned the subject and I'm willing to respect that. Besides therapy, Dad keeps busy learning about heat pumps through the mail. We study together nights, him with his diagrams of condenser coils, me with my genetic charts, hot on the trail of recessive traits. Every other weekend I give him a test, keep the time and watch him for cheating. He hates me for it, but so far he's passed every test.

Mom, she's holding her own as usual, especially since she is the legally designated "responsible supervising adult." She's pretty satisfied with her new job as a "day companion" to some woman named Mrs. Loomis, and it gets her out of the house, so's she's not trapped, as she likes to say. Sometimes I even think she really loves watching over old Loomis and her matched set of Yorkshire terriers. She goes crazy for the deep-pile rugs, the crystal chandeliers, and Loomis's closet full of imported silk caftans. Every day she's got a brand-new Mrs. Loomis story: "Mrs. Loomis and the Freeze-Dried Coffee Explosions," "Mrs. Loomis and the Milk-Drinking Squirrel." Weekends she takes Vanessa over there and they go swimming in the lima-bean-shaped pool after Ness helps with the Yorkies' flea baths. I go, too, some weekends, and vacuum the pool, stuff like that—part of my rehabilitation, I think, and Mom says anyway it teaches responsibility.

My rehabilitation. Mostly it involves Mom dressing me up like a shoe salesman and presenting me on selected formal occasions to Judge Lambesch, who talks to me like

210

I'm a turtle. I answer politely and keep my head inside my shell. He seems satisfied. Pachesky is usually there; he's my probation officer responsible for the day-to-day stuff. He's always at school, talking to my teachers, or paying little visits to Mom. He says he admires her backbone, but I suspect he has his eye on other things as well. Still, he got the kidnapping charge dismissed, and that, as he keeps reminding me, was the "biggest hurdle of all." Last time out he took us to a Dairy-Freeze—that's where your tax money goes—and congratulated us on being a model family. The judge, he told us, has been very impressed with our progress. Mom rewarded him with a tight frozen smile, but when we got back home and I'd gotten down to bare feet and shorts once again, she collapsed across the sofa in tears.

I sat down beside her, kneading the bunched muscles back of her neck. "Easy, Mom, easy. I'm sorry to put this all on you."

"No, it's not that. It's all this pretending. Did you hear what the judge said about a 'model family'? Can you believe he thinks we're a model family? Maybe once we had a chance . . . but—"

"There are no model families," I interrupted, "just a lot of confused mothers and fathers and kids, trying to be whatever they think mothers and fathers and kids should be. And I bet none of 'em got any more clue what to be than we do. You kinda got to make it up as you go along."

"Maybe we just ran out of clues," she said, trapping my free hand between her own. "I know you wanted us to be some kind of family so bad, and look what we are."

"We still can; look at us—all right here. All you have to do is walk next door and say so, say, 'Enough, I'm back; let's get started.' "

"No, Nelson, I can't do that. It's just more pretending, and that's what I've had enough of. You spent the whole summer trying to force us back together—but love doesn't come because our son says, 'Right, now everything's like old times,' because it's not. Sure, we're all back at Gate o' Palms, but it's our prison now, not our home. You can understand that, can't you? A family can't be held captive by its children. You can't kidnap your whole family."

"Sure, Mom, I can see that now." And I could, even if I didn't want to. I could see that Mom and Dad might never be together again; I could see that Vanessa and I might have a mother and father, but no longer parents, no more family. "Sure, Mom," I repeated. "I can handle it."

And still, I am haunted by the thought that with enough time, with enough healing, living side by side through the days, months, just maybe . . . But no, I promised myself I wouldn't say it, so I won't.

Besides, it's really Heidi that haunts me most. Heidi, who's been hidden away at the Florida State Ranch for Girls ever since last September, getting my letters, I suppose, but staying silent. I even called once, but she wasn't "available," I was told, although I did learn that they'd be ready to let her out in two more months since she'd been such a "model resident." The only catch is, she'll never be released until she can find a family or guardian willing to take her in. And that's a serious long shot.

Me and Dad got to discussing her problem and decided the only proper thing to do is take her in ourselves. Dad even says we could adopt her legally—a bizarre thought, to consider that it would make her like my sister, and that would give brotherly love a new meaning. Of course, Dad did develop a fondness for Heidi's spaghetti, and that carries a lot of weight with Dad even if he is still months away from the prospect of tasting tomato sauce.

So far, then, it's still just between me and Dad. Vanessa would probably go along, but if we told her, it wouldn't give us the time we need to work on Mom. But we have a plan, we always have a plan. First Heidi comes down for a weekend and makes a dinner and takes Vanessa skating, or something. Then they get real chummy, and Mom sees how helpful and all Heidi can be. See, she never got to really *know* Heidi, like I did, or Dad, or Vanessa. And maybe after a few of those weekends we just sorta suggest how nice it would be, and then we set Vanessa to work on Mom. Good old Vanessa, she always could just kind of slither her way onto Mom's good side. Dad says the state might pay us 150 bucks a month, and that might sweeten it enough for Mom to soften up to the idea some. It might not hurt to try, is all I'm saying. You never know. . . .

35

Dear Heidi,

First—you don't write me because you hate my guts. You hate my guts because I sprung the trap, and you and the cowboy got snagged. Well, good. That's right, I said good. Because at least now I know where you are. That's important, to know where people are that you really care about. I said really care about. That guy was just a free ride to nowhere. I couldn't let you get away—from me—with him or anybody else. Last summer—you and me—is the only real thing I have. The Gato Family is very touch and go. Maybe it'll work, maybe it won't. Yours didn't, it died long ago. Listen, I think about you all the time. I've got a plan——nothing too crazy this time, but I'm saving it 'til I see you.

Love,
NELSON

Two weeks, three weeks went past and I heard nothing. Finally I sent her a postcard. "I'm coming" was all it said, not even my name.

So I took the bus to the Girls' Ranch. Heidi was waiting in a dress, of all things, which she had stitched together herself. She didn't bother to explain why she never answered my letters, but she looked happy to see me, so I let it drop. She introduced me to her counselor and checked me into the guest house. When we got to my room, the counselor said we could "visit" but I'd have to leave my door open. I guess they didn't want any guests to be sexually molested or anything. But that didn't bother Heidi much. She grabbed me in a hug and smacked me a half-serious kiss on the cheek. I dropped my suitcase on her foot.

"Ow, careful, Nelson. God, I miss your big dumb face. Why don't you grow a mustache? Do you still shave with a weed eater, or are you ravaged by acne? How's Vanessa?"

"Easy, Heidi, I've got all day, slow down." I sat her down on the bed while I unpacked. We filled in the empty spaces since September, and Heidi told me about life at the ranch. It was sort of a motel for problem girls. Everyone worked; every girl had responsibilities. Heidi kept the bulletin board, sorted mail, ran the weekend rec hall program. She was learning to make jewelry, too.

"See, brand new this week," she announced, pulling back her dark curls. Two silver figure eights dangled from her ears.

"Gorgeous, Heidi; they look good on you," I told her. "Even better than those gypsy hoops you used to wear." I meant it, too.

"Nelson, you remember those things. How sweet. That was the day we went to Sarasota with your dad, right?" She was right. Suddenly, we were two old-timers, reminiscing

215

about the good old days. I went on to explain my reason for being there. She was beside herself with joy, but I had to cool her off by telling about our plan to convince Mom.

"I'll be a terrific sister. We can hang out and go to school and it'll be like a real family, you'll see." She asked if I'd heard from her mother, but there was no news. I think the police had given up looking.

"What about the old gang at school? Do any of those greaseballs ever ask about Heidi T?"

"Sure, they all ask about you, almost every week. Old Bernie, and Skate, and J-Boy and Phyllis Caputo, they just can't hear enough." I was lying, of course. No one had ever asked. The old gang had unofficially disbanded.

"Hey, neat. Well, tell 'em all 'hi' for me and tell 'em I'll be down soon, so they better shape up." She stood up and watched out the window. Girls walked the concrete with parents visiting for the weekend. Others sat under the gray branches of oaks talking to boyfriends, their heads bobbing, as they smiled and frowned in unison.

"Guess what, Nelson, you're my first visitor ever," she announced. I had assumed as much, but I kept quiet. "I know what, let's walk over to my room. I want to show you off. Plus I got you a surprise, too, if you're extra good."

She took my arm, very formal, and we strolled painfully slowly across the brown lawn to the dorm where she lived. Along the way she introduced me to everybody, even to a withered old guy in spotty khaki twills that must have been the groundskeeper. To some she said I was a boyfriend from downstate. Others learned I was her brother, the all-state wrestler from Palmetto.

When we got to her room she introduced me to her roommate. "This is the one I've been telling you about," she said. The roommate left and we were alone. The walls

216

were plastered with magazine ads. Mostly guys in jeans and no shirt, that kind of stuff. The beds were scrambled with sheets and pajamas and mangy-looking stuffed animals. One desk had a radio and a circle of snapshots pasted under plastic: a boy on a bike, a gray-haired woman, two girls grinning and pointing to their braces. The other desk, Heidi's, was bare, except for a few schoolbooks and a mess of scribbled-on stationery sprawled across the desk. I recognized the scribbling. It was mine. Some of those letters had been written months ago.

Heidi reached in the bottom drawer of the desk and pulled out something spinning at the bottom of a silver chain.

"Remember this?" she said, dropping the chain in my lap. Attached to the chain was a silver gator, the one with the obsidian eyes Dad had gotten me at Aztec Artisans.

"Sure do; it's my good luck gator. How'd you get it?"

"I sort of borrowed it from you. I lost mine when we got to that ghost town place. I made the chain. Do you like it?"

"Beautiful, looks professional. Is this the surprise you had for me?"

"No, that's mine now. I'm keeping it to remind me of you. You can sort of consider it an unofficial gift from you to me. It's like they say about diamonds: 'A gator is forever.' "

She slipped the chain around her neck and then she reached into the drawer again. "Here's what I made for you after I knew you were comin' up. Now close your eyes and open your hands and promise you won't laugh or throw it away."

I promised both of those things and she slipped something into my palm. It was wrapped in tissue paper, but I

217

could feel hard edges underneath. With my eyes still closed, I unwrapped it and dropped the tissue to the floor. It was flat and hard, and a little cool as I rubbed it under my thumb. I opened my eyes and saw a gleaming silver buckle, polished and shined so that it reflected the light from the naked bulb overhead. It was embossed with letters barely cut into the mirrorlike surface, and when I held it up I expected it to say "Stroh's" or "Coors" or "Raise Hell" or something like that. But when I finally got it focused I recognized Heidi's special backward slant and the two words she had etched across its surface. So when I'm wearing my belt nowadays and I twist the buckle up like this I can still read what she wrote and remember her saying "Go ahead and read it," so I do. And this is what those two words say:

FULL NELSON